The O'Neals In

The Lost Lodge

Michael Slater

The O'Neals In

The Lost Lodge

Michael Slater

2025

Copyright pending

Some illustrations by:

Tia O. Powers
Allison Bandy

Some illustrations used AI assistance

ISBN: 978-1-961482-24-1

Table of Contents

A Note to Parents
A Note to the Reader

A Note to Parents

As a Nationally Certified School Psychologist, I have worked in the field of psychology for well over 40 years, much of that time within the public school system. During those years, I personally administered hundreds—if not thousands—of IQ and educational tests. I have been astounded to find that so many school-aged children are unable to read and write at, or even near, their current grade level.

This detective novel was written both to challenge and to plead with parents: to enhance and develop their child's cognitive abilities while improving academic performance.

It is distressing that so many capable students struggle to read and write at grade level. When administering intelligence tests, I frequently find that many third, fourth, fifth, sixth, and seventh grade students can barely read or write. I recently tested a third grader who did not even know his last name.

What is even more surprising is that these children are not mentally handicapped in any way. I believe many of them have simply not been challenged academically to improve their cognitive and reading abilities. They possess the ability, but have not pushed themselves—or been pushed by parents or school personnel—to grow. All too often, children are allowed to spend countless hours playing video games, watching television, or using computers and phones for entertainment rather than education.

Furthermore, too many parents place a greater emphasis on sports than on academics, nurturing the dream of their child becoming a professional athlete with a multimillion-dollar contract. Parents send their children to sports camps, hire personal trainers, and enroll them in travel teams. Countless hours, out-of-town trips, hotel stays, and other expenses are invested in the hope of giving their child the best chance at a professional sports career.

Please note: your child is highly unlikely to become a professional athlete. The chances of a student athlete going pro are approximately 0.023 percent—far less than one percent. If you were a betting person, would you invest the majority of your child's time and attention in something with a 0.023 percent chance of success? Or would you rather invest in something with guaranteed lifelong benefits? If your child excels academically, he or she is almost assured of a successful and fulfilling career.

A child's brain should be envisioned as a muscle. If you work the muscle—if you challenge it—it becomes stronger and more developed. If you do not, atrophy sets in. The brain becomes weak and underdeveloped, setting the child up for failure in the classroom, limited academic advancement, and possibly a bleak future.

Academics should be viewed as building blocks. A child must first master the foundational "blocks" of the elementary grades before progressing to higher levels. When children fail to master the basics, they become lost when faced with more advanced material. Too many students have missed or failed to grasp those fundamentals; as a result, they are now academically stumped, yet they are socially promoted to higher grades. Inability to understand the material often leads to boredom, which in turn produces disruptive behavior—hindering both their own learning and that of others, while making the teacher's job extremely difficult.

Deficiencies in reading and comprehension affect every subject—science, history, and even math. Yet students are frequently promoted without having mastered the necessary material. Many classrooms I've visited resemble a zoo more than a productive learning environment. I have observed students being unruly, talking out loud, leaving their seats without permission, disobeying or arguing with the teacher, and even showing aggression. Often, the teacher has little or no control over the class.

Many of the IQ tests I administer yield a Verbal Intelligence Quotient

(VIQ). The best indicator of a student's success in college is his or her verbal intelligence. When administering IQ tests, I can always identify avid readers by their higher VIQ scores, which also raise their overall Full-Scale IQ. Therefore, if we produce readers, we produce college-bound students. If we increase a student's likelihood of college success, we also increase the likelihood of success in their chosen career. Thus—the purpose of this book.

To help build a child's verbal intelligence, I have included in each chapter of this book challenging words along with their highlighted definitions, followed by a summary at the end of the chapter. This design should enhance and expand a child's vocabulary, comprehension, and fluency. Reading with an awareness of word meaning is one of the most effective ways to strengthen language skills.

As the author of this detective mystery—which I intend to develop into a series—my background as a former police officer, prison warden, and school psychologist has fueled my fascination with mysteries and criminal behavior. I believe it is vital that young readers have access to wholesome, engaging books. As a school psychologist, I've witnessed the academic benefits that come from reading quality literature. As a former police officer and prison warden, I also recognize the importance of providing youth with positive outlets that challenge their minds and shape their imaginations. What better avenue is there than reading a good mystery?

Michael Slater

A Note to the Reader

Hello, Reader,

You're about to open a story that's more than just a detective mystery—it's a challenge. A challenge to think deeper, read sharper, and grow stronger.

Within these pages, you'll follow clues, unravel secrets, and face situations that will make you stop and think. Along the way, you'll encounter words that may seem new or difficult. Don't skip them— conquer them. Each word has been chosen to stretch your mind and build your vocabulary. The more words you master, the more powerful your thinking becomes.

Strong readers are strong thinkers. Reading trains your mind to notice details, make connections, and solve problems—the same skills detectives use. Every page you read strengthens your brain like exercise strengthens a muscle. The more you challenge yourself, the smarter and more confident you become.

So as you turn the pages, don't rush. Let yourself get caught up in the mystery, picture the scenes, and think through the puzzles. You may just discover that the greatest mystery you're solving is how much potential lies within you.

Now, sharpen your mind, step into the story, and let the investigation begin.

Your fellow detective,
Michael Slater

Chapter I

Fright or Flight

Thirteen-year-old Sydney Reese O'Neal clutched the armrests of her seat until her knuckles turned white. Her ordinarily pink cheeks were now a pale shade of green, intensifying her gray-green eyes and dark lashes. Her normally loose-flowing brown hair clung to her face, now dampened with perspiration.

"Oooh. I think I am going to be sick," Sydney mumbled, trying to keep her breakfast down.

"We haven't even taken off the ground, Sydney! Suck it up!" Josh exclaimed.

"Don't be so *stern* with her, Josh. After all, this is her first flight," Mr. Jake O'Neal said to his older child. He marveled as he looked upon his two children. Josh, fifteen, being the older of the two, was much more self-assured, daring, and confident. At five-ten, he was slender and firm. The short crop of dark hair around his round face accentuated his almond-shaped brown eyes. He thought about how different they were. Sydney was thirteen going on twenty-one and stood five feet four inches tall. She had the beauty and gentle nature of her mother. He sometimes regretted how much Josh took after him.

- **Stern: serious and unrelenting**

Being a private detective was his sideline. After working as a *Clinical Psychologist* for several years, he began to study the new and developing field of *Forensic Psychology*. Jake O'Neal developed a fascination for the criminal mind. This led him to be instrumental in solving many crimes. He was now an *eminent* psychological investigator, and his reputation and popularity soared. He was now known as 'Sherlock O'Neal', and Josh was determined to be his Dr. Watson.

- **Clinical Psychologist:** **an expert or specialist in the branch of psychology concerned with the assessment and treatment of mental illness and psychological problems.**
- **Forensic Psychology: the practice of psychology applied to the law. Forensic psychology is the application of scientific knowledge and methods to help answer legal questions arising in criminal, civil, contractual, or other judicial proceedings.**
- **Eminent: renowned, well-known**

"Dad," Sydney gasped, as the engine revved up, "are you sure this jet is safe?"

"Trust me, flying is safer than riding in a car."

"I mean. we don't know ... who is driving this thing," Sydney argued. "How do we know if he's even got a driver's license?"

"You mean his pilot's license," Mr. O'Neal corrected.

"Well, whatever! But what if he got it by mail or something?"

"Yeah, Sydney, I'll bet he was given his license when he made the high score on a video game which simulates flying planes, or maybe he had to send in five box tops from cereal boxes, after he had eaten the cereal," Josh said *sarcastically*.

- **Sarcastically: in an ironic way intended to mock or convey contempt**

"Oooh... don't mention food," Sydney cried. As the plane climbed into the sky, she could feel her heart hit her stomach. And then the *inevitable* happened. Josh was now wearing Sydney's breakfast.

The Lost Lodge

"Gross!" Josh exclaimed, trying to keep from gagging at the stench. "You barfed all over my shirt and pants! Why didn't you turn the other way?"

"Well, I couldn't very well throw up on Dad! Besides, it's your fault for hogging the window seat."

"Did you have to eat so much? Look at me! I'm a mess!" Josh said.

After a while, Sydney began to laugh hilariously.

"I don't see what's so funny!" Josh said, somewhat annoyed.

"Suddenly, I don't feel so bad. I mean, after the initial take off, this kind of feels like a bus ride. It's not so bad after all. I mean, I really feel kind of silly now. I was afraid for nothing."

"I wish you had come to that conclusion before you decided to share your breakfast with me. Thanks a lot!" Josh said, then stormed off to the restroom with his carry on.

"Dad, you look as though you have a lot on your mind," Sydney said, as she *contemplated* her dad's *somber demeanor*. He had a way of looking straight forward with a cold stare when he was concentrating on something. His thick black brows came together while he stroked his beardless chin. At six feet, three inches tall, he was a handsome robust man, with thick black hair and dark brown eyes.

- **Inevitable: certain to happen; unavoidable**
- **Contemplated: look thoughtfully for a long time at**
- **Somber: dark or dull in color or tone, gloomy**
- **Demeanor: outward behavior or bearing**

"Is it that obvious?" he asked, breaking his silence.

"He was thinking about Mr. Peterson," Josh said as he brushed by them to get back to his window seat.

"Oh! What a horrid smell!" complained a woman sitting in the seat in front of Josh.

"I think she is talking about you," Sydney whispered to Josh.

"I'm so embarrassed. I can't wait to get to Colorado to change my clothes." "How did you know that I was thinking of Mr. Peterson?" Mr. O'Neal said with *astonishment*.

• **Astonishment: great surprise**

"Simple deduction, my dear Sherlock," Josh said mockingly. "Mr. Peterson, an unfamiliar person visits us and all of a sudden, you are taking time out of your busy schedule to take us skiing. Come on, Dad. You are on a case, aren't you? When do we start looking for clues?"

"Okay, okay, maybe you are half right. I am on a case. But 'we' don't look for clues, I do! You two are on vacation, and besides, you are part of my cover. So, keep your noses out of it."

With his head cocked to the right, Josh pulled his eyebrows together and rubbed his chin as he voiced his opinions. "Dad, I was thinking…"

"Oh, you were, were you?" Mr. O'Neal struggled to conceal his grin as he watched his little sleuth mirror him.

"You know, Dad, I don't think Mr. Peterson is a very happy man," Josh said.

"He looked like the jolly fat man to me," Sydney said, filing her fingernails.

"No, he's definitely not happy. He is a man that has really suffered," Josh said, as he continued to stroke his chin, looking forward in a deliberate stare.

"And how do you come to that conclusion?" Jake O'Neal asked.

"It's his face. It's a dead giveaway. Sometime in his life, he was probably a nice looking man. But his *countenance* is so sad," Josh said, drawing a mental picture of him.

Mr. Peterson was a red-headed man of about fifty, his waist well-padded in the middle. His receding hair-line revealed thick creases in his brow, and his lips turned downward. His eyes were dull and empty.

The Lost Lodge

- **Countenance: a person's face or facial expression**

Really, countenance, Sydney repeated in a sarcastic manner, as she rolled her eyes at this. Josh was always trying to use big words when playing Dr. Watson. In fact, Josh would even study vocabulary words and their definitions to improve his verbal expression skills. But Sydney thought it was just so he would look smarter.

"Well Josh, I'll have you know I have been improving myself also. Just like you, I have also been studying vocabulary words, and their definitions. So, we'll see who has the best vocabulary."

"What do you mean?" questioned Josh.

"Like I said, I have been actively studying to improve my vocabulary. So now I will know what all those big words mean when you say them, and furthermore, if you are in fact using them correctly. So, you just better be ware, or I'll call you on it," interjected Sydney.

"Nevertheless, that's a very astute observation, my dear Watson," Jake O'Neal complimented his son.

"Oh! Oh! Oh! *Astute! Astute! That means smart, as a very smart observation*," Sydney said proudly, as she beamed with pride, because she was now able to show off what she had learned. And the best of all, she had beat Josh to the punch.

"You're right. He suffered a great loss when his son died fifteen years ago. He told me about it when he visited the other day." Jake O'Neal began to stare out, rubbing his chin again, as he was going over that visit with Mr. Peterson in his mind. It was playing like a video recorder. Charles Peterson did appear to be a most unhappy man. He had reason to be. He came to Jake O'Neal asking for help. He remembered the conversation well.

It went like this: "Mr. O'Neal, someone is trying to kill me!" he said, wringing his hands together.

"What leads you to believe someone is trying to kill you?"

"I've had phone calls, threatening phone calls." Perspiration began to break out on his forehead. Pulling his handkerchief from his pocket, a crumpled paper fell to the floor.

"What is this?" Jake O'Neal said, retrieving the curious paper.

"This is the latest threat," Mr. Peterson said. With shaking hands, he opened the plain piece of paper with glued letters cut out of newsprint. "Go ahead, read it."

"Your time will end soon. I've hunted you a long time and will soon close in for the kill," Jake O'Neal read aloud. "Do you know of any reason at all that someone would want to see you dead?"

"No, I've never hurt anybody."

"What kind of work do you do?"

"I'm the CEO of Brexler Laboratories. I've worked very hard to attain this position. I suppose I could have made some enemies on the way to the top. You know O'Neal, it's a dog-eat-dog world out there."

"Have you gone to the police with this?"

"Of course I have. But I travel extensively, and the threats have come while I was in three different cities. It's as though someone knows my *itinerary*, as in where I am at all times."

- **Itinerary: a detailed plan for a journey, especially places to visit.**

"So, you think it might be someone in your company?"

"I shudder to think so. But it must be," Mr. Peterson said, with quivering lips.

"So, what is it you want me to do for you?"

"For a year now, we have planned a trip for our top executives to Northeast Colorado. Every year we select a place away from the hustle and bustle of everyday business, so we can catch a fresh vision for the coming year. You know, mix a little business with pleasure. Maybe a little skiing, hunting, and fishing. The trip is scheduled for this weekend. I think this fanatic is going to make his move then."

"Then why don't you just cancel the trip?" Jake O'Neal suggested.

"No, O'Neal, I…I won't be ***intimidated***! I'm no ... co... coward!" he stuttered, mopping his dripping brow. "It's time to flush out this terrorist."

"Well, we don't know what this person's ***stratagem*** might be, so it could get risky."

"I understand! I understand Mr. O'Neal, but I just want this to be over," Mr. Peterson said.

"And you want me to help flush the would-be killer out for you?"

"Exactly!" Charles Peterson said. He then hung his head and sobbed uncontrollably.

"Settle down man, we'll help you get through this," Jake O'Neal said in a manner of ***exhortation***. I promise, I'll see what I can do for you."

- **Intimidated: frighten or overawe, especially to make them do what one wants**
- **Stratagem: a plan or scheme**
- **Exhortation: an address or communication emphatically urging someone to do something**

"Come, let's have some coffee and you can tell when this all started."

Later, as they departed, a more composed Mr. Peterson said, "I do appreciate you taking time out of your busy schedule to meet with me on such short notice. By the way, do you hunt?"

"Why, yes I do, when I can find the time"

"Wonderful! The mule deer hunting up in Northwest Colorado is great this time of year. There's ***abundant*** wildlife in that area."

"A hunting trip would be a good cover for me," Jake O'Neal said. "People won't be suspicious of me. I'll be able to do a little investigating."

"What type of rifle do you use?" Charles Peterson asked, as he made his way to the front door, passing the gun cabinet.

"A Marlin 30-30, lever action."

"So, do I. And what grain bullet do you shoot?"

"I usually stay with a 150 grain."

"So do I. I tell you, Jake, do you mind if I call you Jake?"

"No, go right ahead."

"I tell you, Jake, a lot of people like a bigger rifle or heavier load, but I find the 30-30 rifle to be *inferior* to none. Especially with a 150 grain bullet it is plenty accurate enough, has very little *recoil* or kick, and has all the knockdown power I'll ever need. It just does the job. I look forward to seeing you up there and maybe doing a little hunting with you."

- **Abundant: existing or available in large quantities.**
- **Inferior: lower in rank, status or quality**
- **Recoil: suddenly spring or flinch back**

"Do you hunt much?" Jake asked.

"I, I used to. That is ... when ... my son, Bobby was still alive." The gleam from the talk of hunting left his eyes as he mentioned his son.

"I'm sorry, Charles. I didn't know," Jake said, patting him on the shoulder.

"It's not your fault. It's just that it's been fifteen years, and I still miss him."

"Well, Charles, let's make it a *priority* of ours to get back into hunting and enjoy the great outdoors on this trip."

"Sure, that sounds good to me," Charles stated as he proceeded to the front door. The two men shook hands and departed.

"Dad. Dad. Helloooo!" Sydney said, waving her hand before his staring gaze.

"Yes, what is it, Sydney?" Mr. O'Neal asked, coming back to reality.

"We're here!" Sydney said.

"Come on, Dad," Josh urged. "I've got to get out of these nasty clothes."

The Lost Lodge

The passengers **simultaneously** crowded the aisles, making their way off the plane. A heavy set, somewhat **obese** woman, with equally heavy scented perfume, pushed her way past them. Josh could not help but hear what she said to her husband, all the while glaring at him in disgust. "Poor dear, it's probably not his fault. His father probably never taught him anything about grooming. He probably hasn't had a bath in a week. Humph!" She then looked at Jake O'Neal and said, "Beast!" She threw her scarf about her neck, turned up her nose, and marched off.

"What was that all about?" Jake O'Neal asked, puzzled by the comment.

"It's my aftershave, Dad," Josh said, **humiliated**.

- **Priority: the fact or condition of being regarded or treated as more important**
- **Simultaneously: at the same time**
- **Obese: very fat or overweight**
- **Humiliated: make someone feel ashamed and foolish by injuring dignity and self-respect, especially publicly.**

"What?" Jake O'Neal asked, still confused. Sydney grabbed his arm and escorted him off the plane.

"Come on, Dad. We'll explain it to you in the car," Sydney said, trying to keep from laughing.

Chapter 1 Definitions Review

1. **Stern:** serious and unrelenting
2. **Clinical Psychologist:** mental health professional with highly specialized training in diagnosing and applying psychological knowledge and methods to legal issues
3. **Forensic Psychology:** the practice of psychology applied to the law. Forensic psychology is the application of scientific knowledge and methods to help answer legal questions arising in criminal, civil, contractual, or other judicial proceedings
4. **Eminent:** renowned, well-known
5. **Sarcastically:** in an ironic way intended to mock or convey contempt
6. **Inevitable:** certain to happen, unavoidable
7. **Contemplated:** look at thoughtfully for a long time
8. **Somber:** dark or dull in color or tone, gloomy
9. **Demeanor:** outward behavior or attitude
10. **Astonishment:** great surprise
11. **Astute:** smart
12. **Countenance:** a person's face or facial expression
13. **Intimidated:** frighten or overawe, especially to make them do what one wants
14. **Exhortation:** an address or communication emphatically urging someone to do something
15. **Abundant:** existing or available in large quantities.
16. **Inferior:** lower in rank, status, or quality
17. **Recoil:** suddenly spring or flinch back
18. **Priority:** the fact or condition of being regarded or treated as more important
19. **Simultaneously:** at the same time
20. **Stratagem:** a plan or scheme
21. **Astute:** smart, as a very smart observation

22. **Itinerary:** a detailed plan for a journey, especially places to visit
23. **Humiliated:** make someone feel ashamed and foolish by injuring dignity and self-respect, especially publicly
24. **Obese:** very fat or overweight

Chapter 2

Encounter with a 'Strange' Man

As our three heroes **commenced** their drive to the lodge, they wound   up the slopes in a rented car. They **marveled** at the breathtaking snow-covered mountains. Josh hung his head out of the window, drinking in the scent of pine and fresh fallen snow, the dry, chilling wind **caressing** his cheeks.

"Put the window up, Joshua!" Sydney scolded, pulling her jacket tightly about her neck. "It's freezing back here!"

Mr. O'Neal reached over and pulled him back into the car. "Sydney is right, Josh, roll the window up. It feels like a refrigerator in here. And put your seat belt on. Going up the mountains can be dangerous."

"But Dad, it's just so beautiful here. The breeze feels so ... tingly. I absolutely love it."

Josh was amazed at how the mountain seemed to go straight up on the left side of the car, and yet on the right side the landscape seemed to just **plummet**. "Wow!!! Look at that Dad, it goes straight down, on that side. We are over the treetops on the mountain side and look how deep the snow is down there."

- **Commenced: to begin or start**
- **Marveled: to be filled with wonder or astonishment**
- **Caressing: stroking gently or loving**
- **Plummet: fall or drop straight down at a high speed**

"But it's just like a large **crevasse** in the side of the mountain," Josh said.

" Oh! Oh! **Crevasse means a deep open crack**, like in a mountain side," interjected Sydney proudly. "And that's another one I beat you on."

"Okay, okay, so you know the definition. Big deal," Josh said.

"Well, anyway, you'll both have a chance to enjoy all the snow you want when we get to the lodge. Meanwhile, settle down," Jake O'Neal said.

"What's the name of the lodge?" Sydney asked.

"It's called the Lost Lodge," Jake O'Neal said with a bit of **intrigue** in his voice.

"If it's lost, do you think we will be able to find it?" Josh teased.

"All joking aside, you may not be too far off. As a matter of fact, it is very hard to find. It's not even on the map. The nearest town is Martinsville, which has a population of about fifty people. Martinsville is about one-hundred twenty miles Northwest of Denver. We should be arriving about six o'clock this evening, if the snow doesn't slow us down too much," Mr. O'Neal said.

"What then?" Sydney asked. "What do we do when we get to Martinsville?"

"We'll be met by a guide who will then take us to the lodge by snowmobile, her dad explained."

"Couldn't we just take the car all the way to the lodge?" Sydney asked.

"No, Sydney, the terrain is too rough, and this lodge is so isolated it can only be reached by snowmobile."

After several hours of **arduous** driving up the winding road, they arrived at their destination. The long trip ended with the O'Neals pulling into 'Gary's Greasy Grill.' Martinsville was so small, the city limits could be seen on both ends of the town from the Grill. Across from the Grill was a small service station and grocery.

- **Intrigue: arouse the curiosity or interest of; fascinate**
- **Arduous: involving or requiring strenuous effort; difficult or tiring**

"Well, we're here! I'm *famished*. How about a steak?" Jake O'Neal asked his two children, rubbing his belly.

- **Famished: extremely hungry**

"A steak on a greasy grill? I don't think so!" Sydney said in disgust.

"Yeah, Dad. Don't let Sydney eat. She's never ridden on a snowmobile either. And if she couldn't keep breakfast down on the plane, I'm afraid Gary's greasy grub might slip out too, on the trek up the slopes. I just got cleaned up. I'm not taking any chances. If Sydney eats, I'm not sitting by her on the snowmobile," Josh said, determinately folding his arms across his body.

"It's not like I did it on purpose. Besides, I said I was sorry."

"Look, you two can stay out here in the cold and argue, but I'm going in to get a bite to eat," Jake O'Neal said, walking across the snow-covered parking lot.

"Let's go, I am sort of hungry," Sydney said, hurrying after him.

"You're always hungry," Josh said.

Sydney was shorter than both of them and had to quicken her pace to keep up. The old wooden floor creaked as they walked into the diner. The bell attached to the top of the door kept clanging as Josh fought hard to shut it. The winds howled their resistance, striving to let the bitter cold in.

"Let me give you a hand, young 'un," said a toothless, middle-aged, unkempt man.

"Thank you," Josh said.

Sydney tossed him a sideways grin. He slapped her on the shoulder as she stepped past him, without comment. After forcing the door shut, the wind silenced, calling attention to the cracking and splintering of firewood in the fireplace. Its warmth was inviting.

"Joe Strange, at your service ma'am," the older man said with a country slang, as he pulled the fire-engine red cap off his head, revealing brownish-red, *disheveled* hair, a tattooed black cross below his left ear, and a straggly beard.

- **Disheveled: untidy or disordered**

"Thank you," Josh said politely.

"Ain't nothing," he said, with his toothless grin. "You must be the O'Neals. "

"I'm Jake O'Neal. These are my two children, Josh, my older, and Sydney, my younger." He extended a hand to the stranger.

The Lost Lodge

"Nice to meet you, Mr. O'Neal. I'm the caretaker of Lost Lodge. I was sent here to fetch ya, and bring ya back to the lodge," he explained.

"We were just about to order something to eat. Would you like to join us? My treat!" Jake said, pulling up another chair.

"Join ya'? You bet I'll join ya'. Ain't no better eatin' than Matilda's cookin'," Joe Strange said, as he winked at the overweight, stringy-haired, blonde woman at the counter. "Yep, she's the best cook in these here parts. You better eat up, young 'uns. 'Cuz you ain't gonna' see the likes of this kind of grub at the lodge. There's nothin' better than Matilda's cooking. Why, I think I done put on twenty pounds since I been eatin' here, and it's all right here," Joe said, rubbing both hands on his rounded belly. "It's just more of me to love."

The woman blushed and giggled, and said with pride, "Joe, I think I have an extra piece of my famous apple pie, hanging around."

"With ice cream on top?" Joe asked, licking his lips. "Woman, one day I'm just gonna break down and propose marriage."

"And I just might say yes, Joe," Matilda said and then turned to his three companions. 'Well, what'll it be?"

"What do you suggest?" Jake O'Neal asked.

"Put those menus up, young 'uns. Old Joe is gonna' tell ya' what to get. Matilda, by chance do you have that mouthwatering chicken fried steak, mashed potatoes with white gravy, and corn on the cob with lots of melted butter? If my nose serves me right, I say ya' do," Joe said, pulling in a deep breath, with eyes closed, savoring the *aroma*.

> • **Aroma: a distinctive, typically pleasant smell**

"Why Joe, you say the cutest things," the blushing cook said, smiling at the simple man.

"Sounds good to me," Jake said. "We'll have four orders then."

"And don't forget the apple pie," Joe added, as Matilda walked off to the kitchen.

"And the ice cream," Josh added, agreeing with the old gentleman.

Joe looked at Josh and smiled. He seemed like such a simple man, unrefined, and uneducated. He really butchered the English language, talking in his broken, Southern *jargon*. Yet there was something about him you had to like. His eyes were soft and gentle. He seemed real and down to earth, the kind of person who would give the "shirt off his back" if needed and expect the same from his fellow man.

"But, Dad! We didn't even have a chance to look at the menu," Sydney complained. And we don't know what this stuff might cost.

"Sydney! Don't be rude, and there's no need to be *frugal*, as I will be paying for it," Jake O'Neal *reprimanded* his young daughter.

- **Jargon: special words or expressions that are used by a particular profession or group and are difficult for others to understand.**
- **Frugal: sparing or economical with regard to money or food**
- **Reprimand: a rebuke, especially an official one**

"Sorry, lil' lady. But it wouldn't have done ya' no good, no how," Joe said.

"Why not?" Sydney asked.

"Cuz' there's only one menu." He lowered his voice to a whisper. "And I … I'm shamed to say, I can't read. I get nervous around menus and reading stuff, so I memorized every menu for every day of the week. Ya' see Matilda there? Well, she's sweet on me. And I ain't never told her that I can't read. I hope you lil' guys will keep my secret," Joe said humbly. His cheeks became very red, making his brownish-red hair look even redder. He stood up to take his bright yellow overcoat off then threw it over the back of his chair.

"Well," Jake said, "whether you can read or not, it doesn't *diminish* your recommendation for dinner, so we'll stick with the

26

chicken fried steak."

"You'll never get lost in the snow with that bright, red cap and lemon-yellow coat!" Josh remarked.

"Josh!" Jake O'Neal said, giving his son a disapproving look. "Forgive my children for being so blunt. They are usually very polite."

"Oh that's okay. I don't mind. There's a good reason I wear them there bright colors. When I go huntin', I believe in givin' my prey a fair chance. I want him to know I'm comin'. I ain't no coward who comes without givin' my victim a fair warnin'. It makes the sport better. Don't ya think so, Jake?"

"I can't say I agree with your *philosophy*. I think with their keen senses and their agility in the climate, they already have the advantage. I brought my camouflage wear."

- **Diminish: make or become less**
- **Philosophy: theory or attitude held by someone that acts as a guiding principle for their behavior**

"Ever hunt mule deer?" Joe asked.

"Yes, as a matter of fact, I have. And I'm looking forward to it again."

"Maybe I'll see you up there sometime over the weekend."

"If you don't see Dad, he'll certainly see you!" Josh exclaimed, picking up the bright red hat, pretending to put it on his head.

They all laughed until their attention was drawn to the *savory* aroma coming from the platter Matilda was carrying from the kitchen. Joe Strange was right, Matilda knew how to cook.

"Mmmm.... This is as good as any Texas steak. It melts right in your mouth," Jake O'Neal said, *relishing* the meal, as he began to *devour* his dinner.

"Mr. Strange," Josh asked part way through the meal, "why is the Lost Lodge called by that name? Can you tell us about the Lodge?"

- **Savory: full of flavor, delicious and tasty**
- **Relishing: enjoy greatly**
- **Devour: eat or consume**

"Let the man eat," Mr. O'Neal instructed.

"It's okay. I like a good conversation over a good meal," Joe said. "Actually, I've jest been working at the Lodge for a little better than a year now, since the Lodge was reopened. I moved here from Alabama. You see, I done met Matilda here, on that there Internet. We kinda got sweet on each other, and she done got me a job up at the Lodge so we can do some courting. I was sure once I done sent her a picture of me, she'd throw me back in the water and look for a more handsome fish. But she said I was perfect, jest what she was looking for in a man. I didn't have the heart ta' tell her, it wasn't really me that wrote all those sweet notes to her. It was a friend of mine. Seein' I can't read or write, he helped me. Now, here I am!"

"Internet! Can I check my e-mail at the Lodge? Are there computers?" Sydney asked excitedly.

"If ya' need a phone, young un', ya' better use it now. Cuz' there ain't no phone lines once we leave this place."

"What about cell phones," Sydney asked, desperately.

"No, they ain't no use either. The best we can do, when it does work, is a hand radio. "

"Is there television?" Sydney asked, already knowing the answer.

"Ain't nothing but snow, snow, and more snow, and to answer your original question, lil lady, no, there ain't no internet or computers," the caretaker said between bites. "Well anyways, you wanted to know about the lodge, so I can tell ya' what I done heard. Seems it opened some thirty or thirty-five years ago, way back in the mountains. It was a huntin' lodge and resort. I hear tell that it did real well for a while, and then suddenly, people stop cumin' ." Joe gulped down his milk, wiped his mouth on his sleeve, and continued talking in his country dialect. "I suppose folks didn't take too well to going so far out in the woods. Most folks like to go to resorts close to the highways, and conveniences. But not ole Joe. The further away from the rat race, the better. It's God's country out there. You just wait and see. You're gonna love it or my name ain't Joe Strange. "

"But, how did it get it's name, The Lost Lodge?" Josh asked, *intrigued* by the *unique* speech and mannerisms of this unusual stranger.

- **Intrigued: arouse the curiosity or interest of, fascinate**
- **Unique: being the only one of its kind**

"Eh, it probably ain't true no how," Joe said, reaching for his apple pie.

"Tell us anyway," Jake encouraged him. "It sounds like a good story."

"Well, folks say after a couple of poor seasons, the lodge done closed down. There was jest an ole caretaker that lived at the lodge to keep it up. Folks say he used to come into town for supplies once a week. Then suddenly, he disappeared. He never was heard of since. Some think he died. Some say he was murdered."

"Was his body ever found," Jake asked.

"No, never did find a body, dead or alive. Some tell stories of the place being haunted ever since the ole gent disappeared. It's been some fifteen years now," Joe said, starting on his second piece of pie.

"Haunted?" a wide-eyed Sydney asked, not really sure if she wanted to know the answer.

"Calm down, daughter. There's no such thing as ghosts."

"What kind of stories?" Josh urged Joe to continue.

"Oh, you know the usual. People seein' strange things, hearin' strange noises, lights goin' on and off for no reason. That sort of thing."

"There's got to be a logical explanation, right Dad?" Josh asked, looking to him for reassurance. "Anyway, just how *treacherous* could it really be?"

"That is unless there really is some type of *sabotage* involved in

all of this," interjected Sydney

"That's right, Josh and Sydney. There is always a logical explanation. So don't let it worry your pretty little heads. We'll consider all angles and try to figure out what's really going on," their dad said calmingly.

- **Treacherous: involving deception or betrayal**
- **Sabotage: deliberately destroy, damage, or obstruct**

"How did they say he was murdered," Josh asked, wanting to know more.

"They say he was hunted down like an animal and given to the wolves to eat.

Now, there's the legend of the man-eatin' wolf, who got the taste of human flesh, and now nobody who goes up in those mountains comes back alive. But that's jest a legend. I been up in them there mountains, and as ya' can see, I'm still alive. Maybe he's afraid of my red cap, eh? Course, I keep ole Betsy right by my side jest' in case," he said, caressing his rifle.

"Dad, do you think the disappearance of the caretaker has

anything to do with Mr. Peterson's case?" Josh whispered.

"I just don't know yet, Josh," Jake O'Neal said, contemplating the caretaker's story. "There's a lot of ***intricate*** details we still have to consider, so I just don't know yet."

- **Intricate: very complicated or detailed**

Joe Strange, and the O'Neals bid Matilda goodbye as they all piled into the snowmobile and headed for the lodge. Matilda continued to wave her handkerchief until they were out of sight. As the snowmobile wound   up the slippery slope, the kids resumed their interrogation of Mr. Strange.

"So, have you had a busy season so far?" Josh asked.

"Why didn't ya' know?" Joe Strange asked, somewhat surprised.

"Know what?" Sydney demanded.

"Why, this here is our grand opening," Mr. Strange boasted. "The three of ya's our first guests since we been open."

"But you said you opened a year ago," Sydney added.

"Well ... yes and no...."

"It's either 'yes' or 'no.' It can't be both," Josh said in a way that demanded an explanation.

"Kids, give the man a chance to explain. You two haven't given him a moment's peace since you met him," Jake O'Neal said, coming to the poor man's defense.

"Well, ya see, it's like this. The owner of the lodge hired me a little better than a year ago to fix up the place so it could be reopened. But dang blasted, there was so much work to be done. With all the obstacles in the way, this was the soonest we could open."

"So, we are the first guests to stay here since the lodge has reopened?" Jake O'Neal asked, sounding a bit surprised.

"Yep, that's right," Joe said, proudly. "Tonight is the first night paying guests will stay in the rooms since the lodge closed its   doors some fifteen or twenty years ago."

"Kind of makes you feel warm all over, doesn't it Sydney," Josh whispered.

"A little eerie, if you ask me," Sydney answered a little louder than she meant to.

"What did you say young 'un?" Joe Strange asked.

"Ugh ... ugh ... I said ... I said, 'Here ye, here ye, the O'Neals are the first paying guests,'" Sydney said, her cheeks turning red.

"That lil' gal of yours sure is poetic," the caretaker said to Mr. O'Neal. "I'll bet ya is mighty proud of her."

"Actually, I wasn't aware of just how poetic she was," Mr. O'Neal said, laughing.

Sydney felt hot and flushed, embarrassed by her outburst.

"Be quiet, Sydney, or you'll blow Dad's cover!" Josh whispered, giving her a stern look.

"Who owns the Lodge?" Jake O'Neal asked.

"A man by the name of Robert White bought the place. I figure he's gotta be pretty well to do, if ya' know what I mean. He pays me a pretty good wage. I suppose he bought the place for some tax write off or something, cuz' I really don't see how he could make much money on this place, it being so far from civilization. Why did a fellow like you come out here anyhow?"

"I hear the mule deer hunting is pretty good out in these parts," Jake answered.

"That's for sure. But, what about them kids? Are they the huntin' type?"

"Well, surely not Sydney, she's more into fashion, clothes, and make up. But Josh, now he loves to hunt. In fact, he would stay in the woods all day long if I would let him. Of course, he also loves baseball, football, basketball, and even boxing. I thought I would bring them along to do a little skiing."

"Well, there sure is plenty enough snow for skiing," Joe said with chuckle.

"Will Mr. White be there this weekend?" Jake questioned.

"No, in fact, I ain't never seen hide nor hair of the gent. But he sends in my pay, like clockwork."

As the journey continued, Jake wondered about the owner. This was the first time for paying guests to arrive and the owner would not be there? That was not the way to do business. Certainly he would want to be there to welcome his guests and make sure everything ran smoothly for the grand opening. Maybe Joe Strange was right. It could be the owner was not interested in the Lodge itself but only wanted it for a tax write-off. The big snowmobile bounded uncontrollably up the old mountain road, slipping and sliding through the snow and ice. The small road seemed to almost disappear as it passed through thickets of pine and cedar, *meandering* and working its way around the mountain side.

"Boy, this road sure is rough!" Josh exclaimed, striking his head on the vehicle, as he jostled about.

"Yeah!" Sydney responded, trying to keep her balance. "Mr. Joe, I haven't seen any houses since we left Martinsville. Doesn't anyone live around here?"

"Not a soul," Joe replied. "The nearest house is back in Martinsville, might near fourteen or fifteen miles from the lodge. But don't worry lil' guys. Ole Joe is here to serve ya'. I can get ya' anywhere ya' need to go in this here contraption. Fact is, I'm going back to town in the morning to fetch more guests."

"How many guests are you expecting?" Jake asked.

"Let's see, there's a Mr. Peterson, who heads some drug company, and six of his top dogs. So that makes seven in all."

"They are bringing dogs? What kind? Snow dogs?" Sydney asked, naively, causing everyone to laugh. "What! What did I say?"

"You dummy! 'Top dog' is just an expression!" Josh said, *exasperated* with his sister.

"That's right Sydney. He is saying that Mr. Peterson is bringing six of his top, or most important businessmen with him." Jake O'Neal explained to his daughter, then gave her a *consoling* wink of the eye. " And Josh, don't call your sister dummy."

- **Meandering: following a winding course**
- **Exasperated: intensely irritated and frustrated**
- **Consoling: serving to comfort someone at a time of grief or disappointment**

"Yes sir," Josh replied.

"By the way, Joe, what kind of power do you use, surely not electrical? It must be too far up for power lines," Jake O'Neal inquired.

"We have a large generator that runs off diesel. And we have a furnace for heat, and of course good ole fashion firewood. I must say, over the past few months, we have *accumulated* a huge pile of firewood, and we're gonna' need it cuz' a storm is fixin' to move in sometime tomorrow, and it's gonna' dump a lot more snow, along with some mighty low temperatures and high winds. Hope you lil' guys brought some Long Johns along. Or maybe some Long Janes. Ha! Ha!" Joe chuckled at his own joke. "Don't worry, you'll get used to the cold soon enough."

"I don't think I could ever get *acclimated* to this much cold," Sydney said as the snowmobile edged its way up the mountain road, before she dozed off to sleep, as she leaned against her brother's shoulder.

Josh stayed awake, glued to the *authentic* first-hand stories Joe Strange told in his country slang. Though he was a simple man, he had a lot to share along the way about life and nature, as well as past hunting adventures he had enjoyed throughout his life.

- **Accumulate: to gather or pile up**
- **Acclimated: become accustomed to a new climate or to new conditions**
- **Authentic: of undisputed origin, genuine**

Chapter 2 Definitions Review

1. **Commenced:** to begin or start
2. **Marveled:** to be filled with wonder or astonishment
3. **Caressing:** stroking gently or loving
4. **Plummet:** fall or drop straight down at a high speed
5. **Crevasse:** a deep open crack
6. **Intrigue:** arouse the curiosity or interest of; fascinate
7. **Arduous:** involving or requiring strenuous effort; difficult or tiring
8. **Famished:** extremely hungry
9. **Disheveled:** untidy or disordered
10. **Aroma:** a distinctive, typically pleasant smell
11. **Jargon:** special words or expressions that are used by a particular profession or group and are difficult for others to understand
12. **Frugal:** sparing or economical with regard to money or food
13. **Reprimand:** a rebuke, especially an official one
14. **Diminish:** make or become less
15. **Philosophy:** theory or attitude held by someone that acts as a guiding principle for their behavior
16. **Savory:** full of flavor, delicious and tasty
17. **Relishing:** enjoy greatly
18. **Devour:** consume
19. **Devour:** eat or consume
20. **Unique:** being the only one of its kind
21. **Treacherous:** involving deception or betrayal
22. **Sabotage:** deliberately destroy, damage, or obstruct
23. **Intricate:** very complicated or detailed
24. **Meandering:** following a winding course
25. **Exasperated:** intensely irritated and frustrated
26. **Consoling:** serving to comfort someone at a time of grief or disappointment

27. Accumulate: to gather or pile up
28. Acclimated: become accustomed to a new climate or to new conditions
29. Authentic: of undisputed origin, genuine

Chapter 3

A Mysterious Welcome

It was just about nine o'clock when the snowmobile pulled up at the lodge. The moon was full and bright, revealing the **enormity** of the lodge's structure. The lodge consisted of three stories and was much bigger than the kids had imagined. It was built in a horseshoe shape style and had several outside buildings around it. A large barn with attached stables, which once housed horses, was off to the left. Thick woods encompassed the rear and sides of the lodge, with the parking lot directly in front. Freshly fallen snow blanketed the parking lot, imprinting their path as the three made for the lobby. Lights could be seen coming from windows on all three floors.

"Wow! I'm totally impressed!" Josh exclaimed.

"Yeah, I had no idea the lodge would be this big!" Sydney agreed.

"Yeah, it's so **capacious**. **Capacious, that means roomy**," Josh said, proudly showing off his mental **prowess**.

- **Enormity: the great or extreme scale, seriousness**
- **Prowess: skill or expertise in a particular activity or field.**

"Yeah, yeah big deal," said Sydney.

"You two go warm up by the fire while I check in. And no wandering off, Mr. Joshua. And Josh, that's an order."

"But Dad," he pleaded.

"Don't even think about it. You're on vacation. I do the snooping."

"Mr. O'Neal, we have been expecting you," the clerk said, peering over his wire-rimmed glasses, as Jake O'Neal approached the desk.

"Good evening," Jake O'Neal said politely. He could not help feeling that he knew this man, or that he had seen him somewhere before. He was a proper gentleman, tall and thin, with white hair and a balding spot at the crown. Nothing in his features was very impressive, yet the familiarity was **uncanny**. What a contrast he was to Joe Strange, the caretaker.

"Sign here, my good man," the clerk said, turning the registry to him, pen in hand. "You will be in room 342 and your son in 343, and your daughter will be in the adjoining room 344. Your children's rooms will have to share a bathroom between them. Have you any questions?"

"Yes, where is the elevator, and is there anyone to help the kids with their bags?

I'm sorry, Mister. I didn't catch your name."

"Roberts. Mr. Jonathan Roberts, that is. There is no elevator, and I'm afraid there is no one to assist the young people with their bags. I must man the desk. And Joe Strange is on his way back to Martinsville as we speak, to spend what is left of this gruesome night. He will be retrieving more guests that will be arriving in the morning."

"Just how many employees do you have here? Certainly there must be more than yourself and Joe Strange," Jake O'Neal said.

"But of course," the elderly gentleman replied. "There is the cook, and I might add, a very good one indeed, and two maids. Do you think we need any more staff than that?" The clerk seemed somewhat annoyed at the question. "I think you will find the quality of our service more than *sufficient*."

- **Uncanny: strange or mysterious**
- **Sufficient: enough; adequate**

"Yes, Mr. Roberts, I am sure we will be very comfortable, thank you."

"Your kids seem to be fit as fiddles, in good health, that is. Seeing you have signed them up for skiing, I assume they must be."

"Yes, they are. And they are really looking forward to hitting the slopes."

"Good, then they should have no trouble making it up the stairs with their luggage," the clerk said.

"Is it possible to move our rooms to the second floor?" Jake asked the clerk.

"No, it is out of the question. The second floor is closed for *renovations*. It is locked. The second floor is off limits to guests. Besides, the exercise will do them good. They will need to strengthen their muscles, you know, if they expect to ski. It's a rugged sport, you know. Now get along. It's time to turn in. We have a busy day tomorrow. The stairs are over there. Now shoo!" he said, waving his hand in the direction of the stairs.

Jake O'Neal then went over to the fireplace to meet his kids, wondering about the lights he had seen coming from the second story windows.

- **Renovations: process of improving broken, damaged or outdated structures**

"Sydney, where is Josh?" her dad asked sternly.

"Here I am, Dad," Josh said, before Sydney could answer.

"I thought I told you to stay put, young man."

"But Dad, I had to go to the restroom," he said in his defense.

"Okay, but from now on, I want the two of you together at all times."

"No problem, Dad. This place gives me the creeps," Sydney said, looking around the room. "Look at all the animal heads. You see that big moose head over there? It feels like his eyes are following me."

"Come on guys, get your bags. We'll have to take the stairs to the third floor," their dad said.

"The stairs!" Sydney exclaimed.

"Well, you can stay here and whine, but I'm going with Dad," Josh said, grabbing his things.

"Wait for me, you guys," Sydney said, collecting her luggage.

The stairwell was very dimly lit and cold. As they neared the third floor, wailing noises could be heard below them.

"What's that noise? It sounds like someone crying," Sydney asked, making her way past Josh, causing him to lose his balance and sending his luggage tumbling down the stairway.

"Now look what you made me do. My overnight case! Dad, I told you, we should have left her at home. She's afraid of her own shadow. That noise is just the wind. Now I'll have to go back downstairs to get my bag, thanks to you," Josh complained.

"Guys, I warned you that this was going to be no picnic. You two stay here. I'll get the suitcase," Jake said.

The suitcase had lodged itself against the second-floor stairwell door. As he bent down to retrieve the bag, a flickering light under the doorway caught his eye. He heard footsteps, then they stopped. Voices could be heard coming from the other side of the door. It was the voices of a man and a woman. Straining to hear the conversation, he could make out only a few words. "Honey, the time has finally come. We did it!" the woman said triumphantly. Her voice seemed cruel and *vindictive*. He could also hear a man's voice, but it was fading as they seemed to be walking away from the door. Jake struggled to get a peek through the keyhole. At best, all he could make out was the backside of the woman, who was standing under the lamp in the hall. She had long, shiny, ***platinum*** hair. She was tall and slender, and wearing a silky robe with gold designs on it. The man was concealed by the poor lighting. Then they both seemed to disappear into the darkness. Jake then very carefully tried the door. But to no avail, just as Mr. Roberts had said, it was locked.

- **Vindictive: having or showing a strong or unreasoning desire for revenge**
- **Platinum: precious silvery white metal**

"What took you so long, Dad?" Sydney scolded.

"Calm down, Sydney. Everything is okay. I just had to pick up a few things and put them back into the overnight case. Now, let's get to our rooms. The morning will be here before we know it."

After ***securing*** them in their rooms, Jake O'Neal bade his kids goodnight. "Now, you kids don't have to be afraid. I'll be right across the hall. Like I told you, just whistle if you need me. I'm a light sleeper. I'll be over in a moment flat." He then gave them a hug and headed for the door. Then, with an afterthought, he turned to Josh and said, "Okay, let me have it, Dr. Watson."

- **Secure: fixed or fastened so as not to give way, become loose, or be lost**

"Have what?" Josh said innocently.

"I know you went to snoop downstairs, when you supposedly went to the bathroom. So, what did you find?"

"Well, Dad," Josh said, tilting his head to the right, causing his hair to fall toward his shoulder, "this is a really strange place. I don't think anyone has ever used that bathroom. There was no toilet paper or paper towels to be found. The place was immaculate. There was not a magazine, vending machine, or any kind of sign to make you feel welcomed. It's like the whole place is set up just for us."

"And seven other people," Sydney added.

"Well, you know, it is the grand opening. They probably have a lot of kinks to iron out. Besides, we did come a day early. You guys, get some sleep now. Don't open the door for anyone. I'll wake you in the morning." Jake O'Neal then went to his own room. Sydney was scurrying about the room, looking wildly in all the drawers as if for a lost treasure.

"What are you doing?" Josh asked.

"I'm looking for a Bible. I know there's one somewhere in here."

"What makes you think you'll find one here?"

"The *Gideons* put them in all the hotels. Didn't you know that? When I find it, I'm going to put it under my pillow."

- **Gideons: international interdenominational organization whose activities include placing Bibles in hotel rooms**

"I think they intend for you to read it, not to sleep with it."

"I'll read it too, if I can find it."

"This place is not even on the map. And I don't think it is classified as a hotel. I doubt even the Gideons could find it. But all the same, here, I packed mine. It's the one Mom gave me the night she died. I take it with me everywhere. It makes me feel like I have a part of her with me. You can sleep with it if you want. Now, let's get some sleep," Josh said.

"Thanks, Bro. You know, you can be really great when you want to," Sydney said, clutching the Bible to her chest. She then climbed into the massive bed pulling the crisp cold linens about her neck, yawned, and closed her eyes as if asleep, still clutching the Bible.

Josh could not resist taking one more look around before retiring to his room. When he was sure Sydney was fast asleep in her room next door, he slipped out of his room, locking the door

The Lost Lodge

behind him. The hall was dark, illuminated by an occasional wall lamp and his own small flashlight. He looked at the numbers on the doors, trying each doorknob as he passed by. When he came to Room 331, he could hear clanging noises within. Putting his ear against the door, he could hear footsteps approaching the door. He quickly put out his light and retreated into the shadows around the corner. No sooner had he withdrawn, when the door flew open. His heart beat so rapidly it was taking his breath away. A cold sweat came over him, while his head became very light. He feared if he didn't sit down, he was going to pass out. He fought desperately to slow his breathing, lest the loudness of his panting would cause him to be discovered. The footsteps were moving away from him. Mustering up enough courage, he peered around the corner to see who it was coming out of Room 331. It was a woman. She was not wearing street clothes, but a night gown and robe. If the O'Neals were indeed the only guests, who was this woman, Josh wondered. His heart was beating at normal pace again. He decided he had had enough adventure for one night. As quickly and as quietly as he could, he slipped back into his room and into his bed. His thoughts went back to the woman. Who was she. Could she have been a guest who checked in later? Was she one of the maids? Should he tell Dad about it in the morning? All these questions played on his mind, as his eyes got heavier, and heavier, and finally he drifted off to sleep.

Meanwhile, Jake O'Neal lay on his bed thinking of the day's events. He kept seeing the faces flash before him, Mr. Peterson. Joe Strange. Matilda. Mr. Roberts. The two voices in the hall of the second floor. And lastly, he could hear the voices of his kids echo through his mind. "It's as if the whole place was set up just for us and seven more."

Chapter 3 Definition Review

1. Capacious: roomy
2. Enormity: the great or extreme scale, seriousness
3. Prowess: skill or expertise in a particular activity or field.
4. Uncanny: strange or mysterious
5. Sufficient: enough; adequate
6. Renovations: process of improving broken, damaged or outdated structures
7. Vindictive: having or showing a strong or unreasoning desire for revenge
8. Platinum: precious silvery white metal
9. Secure: fixed or fastened so as not to give way, become loose, or be lost
10. Gideons: international interdenominational organization whose activities include placing Bibles in hotel rooms

Chapter 4

Rise and Shine

The kids were both roused from deep slumber by a knock at each of their doors.

"Sydney, Josh! It's Dad. Time to get up!"

"What time is it?" Josh yelled, still dazed with sleep.

"I don't know, but it feels like I just closed my eyes," Sydney called out.

"Guys, is everything okay?"

"Yes, we're okay," they said in ***unison***.

- **Unison: simultaneous performance of action or utterance of speech**

"It's time to rise and shine. Get out of bed. It's six o'clock. I'll be back in thirty minutes to take you both to breakfast."

"Thirty minutes! Dad, I'll never be able to do my hair in thirty minutes," Sydney said, horrified at the thought.

"For goodness sakes, Sydney, you will be wearing a ski cap," Jake O'Neal replied.

"Yeah, who's going to see us, anyway? We're out in the middle of nowhere," Josh said, stretching. He yawned, stretched again, then quickly jumped out of bed. "I've got the shower first!"

"No fair!" Sydney complained, struggling to get out of the bed.

Mr. O'Neal was back in thirty minutes as he promised.

"I'll be ready in a minute, Dad," Sydney yelled from the bathroom.

"A minute? I guess that means she'll be ready in fifteen. That'll give me ample time to talk to you about something, young man."

"You need to talk to me about something, Dad?" Josh answered, avoiding eye contact.

"I thought I told you not to leave your room last night."

"Dad, how did you know?' Josh asked without even trying to *refute* his dad's **allegation**. He knew he was caught red handed. It was **uncanny** how his dad seemed to know what he was up to, even before he actually did.

"Simple. I placed a piece of ***Scotch Tape*** at the top of the door when I left your room last night. This morning, it was broken."

- **Refute: deny**
- **Allegation: a claim or assertion that someone has done something illegal or wrong, typically one made without proof.**
- **Uncanny: strange or mysterious, especially in an unsettling way**
- **Scotch Tape: transparent adhesive tape**

"Hey, that's no fair! But, how did you know it was me and that Sydney didn't go out through my room? You do realize we have adjoining rooms?"

"That was simple too. Sydney is too scared to go out. And I'm all too familiar with your curious nature. If your mother was alive today, I don't know if she would have approved of how I have reared you kids."

Josh went over and put his hand on his father's shoulder. "Dad, we haven't turned out so bad. We don't do drugs or alcohol. We go to church on a regular basis. We do our homework and make fairly good grades. We do our chores. Well, most of the time. I think Mom would be proud of you and us too. You miss her, don't you, Dad?"

"Yes, I do. I've tried to keep you kids with me as much as possible. Your mom made me promise to do that. But I don't think she had this in mind. I never intended to put you kids in any danger."

"Don't worry, Dad. We have learned an awful lot in the last few years. 'Caution' is our middle name."

The Lost Lodge

"Speaking of caution, why did you leave the room last night?"

"Well, I thought, since we were the only guests, I would try the other doors to see if any were open. You know, to look for clues," he said, sitting at the edge of the seat, his pupils *dilated* with excitement as he *conveyed* the happenings of the night before.

"Are you sure it was Room 331 that the woman was coming out of? Was she a blonde? Was her robe white with gold designs?"

"I am sure it was Room 331, and I am sure it was a lady with long blonde hair, wearing a white robe. But whether or not it had gold designs, I don't know. It was dark.

How did you know she was wearing a white robe?

"Do you remember when I went to *retrieve* your overnight case that had fallen to the second story in the stairwell?"

"Yes, I remember," Josh said, paying close attention to his father's words.

"I saw the same woman then."

"You saw her in the stairwell?"

"No, I heard voices coming from the second floor, behind the stairwell door,"

Jake O'Neal explained.

"But Mr. Roberts said the second floor was locked for *renovations*!" Josh said.

- **Dilated: make or become wider, larger, or more open**
- **Conveyed: communicate a message or information to another, transport or carry to a place**
- **Retrieve: get or bring something back**
- **Renovations: to restore to a former better state**

"Well, it is locked. But I don't know about the renovations. As I peered through the keyhole, I saw the same lady that you saw go into one of the rooms."

"You said you heard voices. Who was she talking to?" Josh asked, his curiosity rising.

"It was a man. That's all I know. His voice was much lower than the woman's. It was barely a mumble."

"Could it have been Mr. Roberts?" Josh asked, wanting answers.

"No, I don't think so," Jake O'Neal *surmised*. He couldn't have gotten up the stairs before us, even if there was another stairwell. He's too old and *feeble*."

- **Surmised: suppose that something is true without having evidence to support it**
- **Feeble: lacking physical strength, especially as a result of age or illness**

"Unless … unless there is an elevator," Josh offered.

"That's a definite possibility. I'll have to check into it."

"And, it couldn't have been Joe Strange. He left for Martinsville last night. But … we never actually saw him leave, did we?" Josh added.

"No, we didn't," Jake O'Neal said, rubbing his chin. His brows were drawn together as he gazed ahead with a deliberate stare.

Suddenly, the bathroom door flung open as a revived and refreshed Sydney announced, "Okay, I'm starving. Let's go to breakfast!"

Chapter 4 Definitions Review

1. Unison: simultaneous performance of action or utterance of speech
2. Refute: deny
3. Allegation: a claim or assertion that someone has done something illegal or wrong, typically one made without proof.
4. Uncanny: strange or mysterious, especially in an unsettling way
5. Scotch Tape: transparent adhesive tape
6. Dilated: make or become wider, larger, or more open
7. Conveyed: communicate a message or information to another, transport or carry to a place
8. Retrieve: get or bring something back
9. Renovations: to restore to a former better state
10. Surmised: suppose that something is true without having evidence to support it
11. Feeble: lacking physical strength, especially as a result of age or illness

Chapter 5

The Seven Arrive

The lodge's restaurant was small, but cozy. The cracking of the fire seemed to play a symphony as the flames danced rhythmically in a variety of colors: red, blue, yellow, and orange. There were several tables covered with white linen, adorned with centerpieces made from pinecones. The large eastern window revealed a picturesque view of the unblemished snow-covered mountains. The atmosphere seemed much different than the night before.

"Good morning! I'm Sarah, your cook and waitress. Find yourselves seats, and I'll be right back with breakfast." She was a middle aged, rounded woman. Her short, brown, curly hair gave her a youthful appearance. Freckles could be seen through her makeup. Her cheerful countenance looked somewhat out of place for this strange lodge. It was evident that she enjoyed her job. "Coffee with cream and two sugars," she said, serving Mr. O'Neal.

"How did you know that?" Jake O'Neal asked with amazement.

"Listen honey, when you work tables as long as I have, you get an eye for folks. Take these two young people, for example. They are not your everyday coffee drinkers. Maybe an occasional café au lait, but I think hot chocolate, with marshmallows, would just hit the spot this morning. Am I right?"

"Sounds great!" they said in unison.

As Sarah left the room, Sydney added, "She is a very affable person. *Affable! That means friendly, good natured, easy to talk to.*"

She was soon back with bacon, eggs, toast, grits, and lots of butter and jam. "Is there anything else I can get you?" The plump cook asked. "Speak up now, don't be shy. In a little while, I'm going to be really busy. Seven more guests should be arriving directly."

"Seven more guests?" Jake O'Neal asked, trying to sound surprised.

"Yes, some businessmen are coming in for some kind of meeting, I hear. Who knows? Maybe they will have a son or daughter come along," she said, winking at the kids.

Sydney *erected* her posture and began to pat her hair in place.

They weren't long into their meal when Mr. Roberts escorted the newly arrived guests to the breakfast room. "Make yourselves comfortable, my good gentlemen. I will have Joe Strange put your luggage in your rooms. Sarah, the cook, will be right out with your breakfasts. Enjoy your stay," Mr. Roberts said, face stiff and starched. The seven businessmen had no sooner been seated when Sarah came out with coffee and orange juice.

"Look Dad," Josh whispered. "There's Mr. Peterson."

Mr. Peterson was conversing with some men around a large round table. They all seemed to be men in the fifty to sixty-year-old range, all but one, who appeared to be in his twenties, and quite handsome at that. Sydney could not help but notice. Maybe one of them did bring a son or daughter, just as Sarah had suggested.

"They don't look anything like murderers to me, especially that young one in the blue ski suit," Sydney offered her opinion while finishing up her breakfast.

"So, what is a murderer supposed to look like?" Josh asked sarcastically.

"Ugh, um!" Jake O'Neal cleared his throat, then changed the subject. "Are you kids ready for a little skiing? Why don't you go upstairs and get ready. I'll pick you up in thirty minutes. "

The two departed for their room while Jake O'Neal took his second cup of coffee to the fireplace. As the men were finishing up their meal, Mr. Peterson excused himself and walked to the fireplace.

"How's the fire?" he asked *jovially*.

- **Erected: constructed an upright structure**
- **Jovial: characterized by good humored cheerfulness and conviviality: jolly**

The Lost Lodge

"Feels good," Jake said, extending his hand to the newcomer. "How do you do? I'm Jake O'Neal."

"Charles Peterson, nice to meet you. Are you here for some skiing?" Mr. Peterson asked, pretending not to know Mr. O'Neal.

"Maybe some," he said, loud enough for others to hear. "What room are you staying in, Peterson?" Jake O'Neal whispered.

"Room 331. Why do you ask?"

"That's what I was afraid of. Have you been in the room yet?"

"No, we were picked up early this morning in Martinsville. We were brought directly to breakfast. Our bags are being placed in our rooms. We will be taken to our rooms after breakfast. "

"Stall them. I need to check out the room. Do you have a key?"

"Yes."

"Give it to me. I'll get it back to you," Mr. O'Neal continued to whisper, taking the key.

The rest of the men began to gather around the large *hearth* while Sarah served more coffee.

• **Hearth: the area in front of a fireplace**

"So, you came up for mule deer hunting," Mr. Peterson said, loudly.

"Yes. And of course, I promised my daughter and son some skiing," O'Neal said.

"I'm glad to meet a fellow skier," the youngest of the gentlemen said. "Hi! I'm Bill Clark."

"This is Jake O'Neal. He's from Louisiana. He works as a Psychologist in the prison system there. We've been talking about the mule deer hunting here," Mr. Peterson said, sounding very convincing.

"I'm actually more into hunting than skiing. But I've been promising my kids a ski trip for some time."

"I used to be a ski instructor. That's how I worked my way through college. I'd be happy to take your kids skiing if you would rather do some hunting"

"Thanks, Bill. I'll keep that in mind," Mr. O'Neal said, wondering at the *amiability* of this young, muscular man. He had dark hair that swept to the side, with bright blue eyes. His half smile revealed a dimple on the right side of his cheek.

"Mule deer hunting sounds good," another man said, as he approached the hearth.

He was tall and slim, with blonde hair and fair complexion. His feet seemed somewhat large for his frame.

"O'Neal, meet Frederick Moore, the 'quick-draw' of the South," Bill said. "Now, if you want a little competition, this is your man."

"I'm afraid he's flattering me. Although I do like a little competition. Would you like to wager a bet on who gets the first deer? They don't call me 'quick-draw' for nothing," Moore said.

"I like the sport but no thanks. I'm not a betting man," Jake O'Neal said.

"Wise choice, man. He'll show you no mercy. He'll take you for everything you've got. He's a *shrewd* one," said an *obese* balding man.

"You're a fine one to be talking, Carl," Mr. Moore said. "You should have the title of 'quick-draw,' not me."

"So, you're a pretty good shot, too?" Jake O'Neal asked. They all laughed at the comment. "What's so funny?"

"Just the thought of Carl Young with a gun is funny. He's very *benign* and also anti-gun," Bill Clark said.

- **Amiability: the quality of having a friendly and pleasant manner, geniality**
- **Shrewd: having sharp powers of judgment; astute**
- **Obese: grossly fat or overweight**
- **Benign: gentle and kindly**

"But, you called him 'quick-draw,' O'Neal said.

"That's right. But it's cards, not guns. I can deal a mean poker hand. Are you interested O'Neal?" The short, fat man then reached into his jacket pocket, pulled out a cigar, and began chewing on it.

"Like I said, I'm not a betting man. But thanks for the offer."

The last three men then rose from the table to join the others at the fire.

"Hey, you guys, this is Jake O'Neal. He's a prison Warden from Texas," Bill Clark said.

"A *Criminal Psychologist*," Jake corrected.

"Well, anyway. This is Thomas Stevenson, Scott McCauley, and Paul Pierce," Bill said.

"Are you all huntsmen?" Jake asked, extending his hand to each one.

"I'll say we are. We're all members of the same hunting club. All but Peterson, and of course, Carl Young. He wouldn't know what to do with a gun, even if his life depended on it," *chided* Thomas Stevenson.

- **Criminal Psychologist: a professional that studies the behaviors and thoughts of criminals**
- **Chided: chastise or make fun of to get someone to change**

Jake studied the three men standing before him. It was uncanny how much they looked like one another. They were all short in stature, standing between five-feet-five inches to five-feet-seven inches tall. They all had thick, curly, graying, black hair, and thick, unkempt mustaches. Jake O'Neal couldn't help but think of the three musketeers as he studied them.

"So, what does a Criminal Psychologist do?" Scott McCauley asked.

"We try to get to the root problem of the criminal mind," Jake explained.

"A frustrating job, I'm sure," Paul Pierce added.

"Don't you think that there is a little criminal in all of us?" Carl

Young asked.

"That's a very strange thing to say!" Mr. Peterson exclaimed.

"I think he's right. I mean, haven't you ever tried to think of the perfect crime?" Fred Moore said, shifting back and forth on his large feet, while being somewhat *ambiguous*.

- **Ambiguous: unclear**

"Yeah, and this would be the perfect place for the perfect crime," Thomas Stevenson said jokingly. "We're out in the middle of nowhere." The men broke out into laughter as they watched Thomas Stevenson doing his imitation of a boy over a campfire telling ghost stories. Charles Peterson looked scornfully upon him, not amused at all by his boyish play.

"What do you think Mr. O'Neal? Is there a little criminal in all of us?" Carl Young repeated his question.

"I really would like to answer that question. But I'm afraid I need to meet my children now. Perhaps later, when I have more time."

"How about joining us on a hunt this afternoon, O'Neal, after lunch," Mr. Peterson invited Jake. "We're going to have a short business meeting this morning. Then we will be ready for some fun and relaxation after lunch."

"I'd like that very much. Is everyone going?" Jake asked.

"I'm out. I think I'll take a nap," Carl Young said, rubbing his large belly.

"I'm hitting the slopes with the skis," Bill Clark said, looking out the window. "You couldn't have picked a better spot, Carl. It's great out here."

"So then have you been out here before, Carl?" Jake asked, trying to get information.

"No, the brochure that came over my desk just looked irresistible. It was my turn to choose the place for the company trip, and the price was right."

The Lost Lodge

Jake O'Neal excused himself, leaving the men to have their meeting. As he walked up the steps, he sorted the clues he had gathered. It was Carl Young who had chosen the Lost Lodge for the company. A man who neither hunts nor skis, chose a hunting and ski lodge for his vacation. Something just didn't add up.

Chapter 5 Definitions Review

1. **Affable: friendly, good natured, easy to talk to**
2. **Erected: constructed an upright structure**
3. **Jovial: characterized by good, humored cheerfulness and conviviality: jolly**
4. **Hearth: the area in front of a fireplace**
5. **Amiability: the quality of having a friendly and pleasant manner, geniality**
6. **Shrewd: having sharp powers of judgment; astute**
7. **Obese: grossly fat or overweight**
8. **Benign: gentle and kindly**
9. **Criminal Psychologist: a professional that studies the behaviors and thoughts of criminals**
10. **Chided: chastise or make fun of to get someone to change**
11. **Ambiguous: unclear**

Chapter 6

A Close Call

Josh peered through the crack of his bedroom door. He watched as Joe Strange delivered the luggage to each guest's room. It took him quite a while since he used the stairs and had many bags to deliver. He had counted seven trips and seven rooms. He was certain he was finished.

"Come on, Sydney. Let's go," Josh whispered.

"Where are we going? Dad told us to stay put, and he would come for us."

"If I know Dad, he's going to meet everyone and try to get some clues. We can help. We can search the rooms. Let's start with 331. There is something strange about that room. I want to see who is staying there."

"Are you crazy!" Sydney exclaimed. "What if we get caught?"
"We won't! Not if we hurry. Come on."

"No! Not in a million years! No way!" Sydney said *emphatically*.

- **Emphatically: in a forceful way**

"Okay, now if you hear anything, remember, two knocks on the door. If you see anything ...," Josh instructed.

"Yeah, yeah. I got it. Now go ... hurry! I can't believe I'm doing this!"

Sydney walked lightly up and down the dark corridor as Josh slipped into Room 331. Strangely enough, it was not locked. He had gloves on so as not to leave fingerprints. He saw only the expected: a clean room, a freshly made bed, and empty drawers. The closet was empty except for the rifle that was still in its case. There was nothing out of the ordinary. A large, camel-colored suitcase lay neatly on the luggage seat near the closet. The tag revealed that this was Mr. Peterson's luggage. Trying the lock on the suitcase, he found it easy to open. To his surprise, Mr. Peterson had very little clothing packed. The poor man was so nervous, Josh thought, it was amazing he managed to pack anything. There were two brand new camouflage hunting outfits, long johns, heavy boots, pajamas, several pairs of socks, and a few personal items. Josh picked them up one by one: a comb, toothbrush, toothpaste, and a full bottle of shaving lotion, although no razor. He quickly and carefully made his way to the bathroom. It was completely empty. The room was *immaculate*, except for two strands of long blonde hair in the bathroom sink. He carefully picked them up, put them into a plastic bag, then secured them in his pocket as he had seen his dad do on occasion. He thought back to the night before. Who was the blonde he had seen leaving the room? It was apparently her hair. What was she doing here? Did she plant something here that could harm Mr.Peterson? Was someone here in the hotel a part of the plan to murder Mr. Peterson?

- **Immaculate: perfectly clean, neat, tidy**

Suddenly the door flung open, startling Josh. It was Sydney. She was white as a sheet. Her breathing was so rapid she couldn't speak. She could only motion with her hands.

"What is it, Sydney? Did you hear something?! Is someone coming?!" Josh demanded, shaking his sister. "Tell me!"

Sydney nodded her head up and down wildly. She was speechless with fright. Then the sound of large rapid footsteps could be heard coming down the corridor.

"Quick, follow me, and don't make a sound." Josh frantically crawled under the bed, dragging his sister with him. Sydney's breathing was loud and rapid. "I mean it Sydney Reese. Don't make one sound!" Josh scolded, pulling Sydney close to him with one hand and covering her mouth tightly with the other.

Suddenly the door flew open. Josh could feel Sydney's tears

running onto his hand, making it difficult to keep his hand from slipping. Sydney's breathing was now very unsteady. Josh continued to hold her tightly, afraid of being found out. He could tell by the sound of the movements, that it was someone lighter and swifter than Mr. Peterson. He was obviously searching the room. Josh tried his best to get a peek of the intruder. He calculated the steps it would take him to reach the closet, taking the chance that his back would be to him. He counted one, two, three, then very carefully lifted the bedspread, loosening his grip on Sydney. He could see blue ski pants. The room was dim, but he knew who the intruder was. It was the youngest of the men that had come with Mr. Peterson. But what was he looking for? Was he the murderer? He looked so honest and was so friendly. What a disappointment, Josh thought.

After a few minutes, the intruder left as quickly as he had come in. When the door closed behind him, Josh motioned to Sydney to be silent a little longer as he slowly eased out from under the bed to check out the situation. Assured of the trespasser's departure, he searched the room once again to see if anything was missing or had changed. As far as he could tell, nothing had changed, except the shells in the gun case. They were now upside down. Everything else appeared the same. He then went back to the bed to retrieve his sister, when he saw a trail of water coming from under the bed. "Sydney! You didn't!" Josh whispered.

The terrified sister could no longer hold in her emotion. She began to cry violently. The fear of the ordeal had caused her to wet her pants. "I'm sorry, Josh, I couldn't help it!"

"Quick! We need to clean up this mess and get out of here. Now, you go to our room and get our towels to replace the ones I'm going to use here." Josh quickly went to the bathroom to get the towels and came back empty handed. "That's strange," he said. "There are no towels."

"What are we going to do?" Sydney asked hysterically.

"Give me your jacket."

"My what?"

"Your jacket! "

"My new jacket?!"

"Well, then give me your pants!"

"I can't give you my pants!"

"Well then, give me something, or I'm going to leave you with this mess!" Josh argued, heading for the door.

"No! Wait! Here, you can have the jacket."

Josh cleaned the area swiftly, being certain not to leave any sign of their presence behind. Once back inside their room, they both threw themselves backward on the bed and breathed a sigh of relief.

"That was close, wasn't it Josh?"

"You can say that again! I was pretty scared myself. But you know what really amazes me?"

"What's that?" Sydney asked.

"Well, this was indeed an *aberration*," Josh said.

"What do you mean?" questioned Sydney.

Josh continued, "Aberration, which means a departure from the normal. So how, in the light of your concern for fashion, did your fear seem to fall away!"

"Oh! My clothes! You're right ... they're wet!"

Josh laughed as Sydney ran to the bathroom to rinse out her clothes.

Chapter 6 Definitions Review

1. **Emphatically: in a forceful way**
2. **Immaculate: perfectly clean, neat, tidy**
3. **Aberration: departure from the normal**

Chapter 7

Searching for Clues

"Now, let's not jump to any conclusions," Jake O'Neal said to his children.

"But Dad, we saw him. It's that young guy in the blue ski suit. The one that came in with Mr. Peterson," Sydney exclaimed.

"The young man you are speaking of, his name is Bill Clark. You were under the bed. Did you actually see his face?" Mr. O'Neal asked.

"Well , no. But we saw the blue ski pants. And I'm pretty sure the shoes were the same," Josh answered.

"Pretty sure is not good enough. There are still many questions to be answered.

Like, why?" Dad said.

"Was Bill Clark in your sight the whole time you were downstairs?" Josh asked.

"Well, there was a time he excused himself. He said he needed to wash his hands," Jake said thoughtfully. "Mr. Peterson is going to hold a short impromptu meeting with the men in the diner. It won't be long because it wasn't scheduled, and they don't have their briefcases with them. I need to take a quick look at the guests' rooms. But I should have ample time seeing I only have six rooms to search now, thanks to you two."

"Can I help, Dad?" Josh pleaded.

"I think you've done enough for one day."

"But Dad," Josh continued to plead, following after him.

"Wait for me! I'm not staying here by myself," Sydney said, trailing behind. Mr. O'Neal headed for Room 332, directly across from Mr. Peterson's room.

"Why are we starting here?" Josh asked.

"Just a hunch," Mr. O'Neal said, trying the lock. "It's open."

"What are we looking for?" Josh asked, eager to help.

"I'm not sure. You just keep watch, and I'll do the looking," Mr. O'Neal said, entering the room.

"Sydney, you keep watch. I'm going to help Dad. If you hear anything, knock twice then go back to our room," Josh instructed, then quickly entered the room before Sydney could protest.

Once inside, Mr. O'Neal found what he was looking for, a black briefcase with the initials C.J.Y. This was Carl Young's room. Mr. O'Neal skillfully picked the lock, then carefully went through the papers until he found what he was looking for. Satisfied with what he found, he folded the paper, slipped it into the inner pocket of his shirt, very carefully locked the briefcase, and exited the room.

"Let's go, Josh. We've got to hurry!" Mr.O'Neal said.

"What did you find?" Josh asked, his curiosity aroused.

"I'll tell you later. You want to help?"

"You know I do," Josh said eagerly.

"Then you take rooms 335, 336, and 337. Take Sydney with you. That way you can cover more ground. I will take 333 and 334. We only have about fifteen minutes. Let's look at our watches. We need to be back here in fifteen minutes, no more. Now, let's hurry!" Mr. O'Neal then patted his kids on the shoulders and smiled, much like a coach sending new players into a game at a crucial time. He had faith in them.

Room 333 revealed to be Bill Clark's room. It was evident by his youthful attire. Going through his personal things, Jake O'Neal came across a diary of sorts. It was in some kind of code. He was familiar with this kind of journal. It was used to track someone's whereabouts and happenings. He quickly jotted down the coded messages and finished searching the room. He would have to crack the code later. Could Bill Clark be the one stalking Mr. Peterson? What was he doing with this kind of journal? Was he indeed the man the kids had seen in Charles Peterson's room earlier?

Meanwhile, Josh and Sydney searched room 335. They came upon a suitcase with Thomas Stevenson's name on it. As it was not locked, Sydney went through his clothes and personal things. Nothing particularly stood out to her. "What are we looking for, Josh?"

The Lost Lodge

"Anything! A murder weapon. I don't know. But we will know it when we see it.

Keep looking. And let me know if you see anything strange."

"What are you doing?" Sydney asked.

"I'm trying to pick the lock on this briefcase. What does it look like I'm doing?"

"Be careful you don't break it," Sydney warned.

"I've been practicing at home. I'm getting better."

"Yeah, I know. But you have broken three picks in the locks of our bicycle chains in the last month. I've had to go to a combination lock because of you."

"Well, if you wouldn't keep losing your key, I wouldn't have to pick the lock. But you will probably forget the combination, and I'll have to pick it again," Josh said, struggling with the lock. "I got it!" he said *exuberantly*. "Let's see what's inside. Sydney!

Get a load of this!" Josh exclaimed, as if finding a hidden treasure.

Sydney went pale as Josh showed her the book that had been concealed in the briefcase. "How to commit the perfect crime!" Sydney read the title, a cold chill ran up her spine as she held the book in her hand. The book's cover alone was the *epitome* of wickedness. The pages were worn as if it had been read over and over again. "What kind of man would read a book like this," she said, hurling it back into the briefcase as if it were *venomous* and she was escaping its poison.

- **Exuberantly: filled with a lively energy and excitement**
- **Epitome: a person or thing that is a perfect example of a particular quality or type**
- **Venomous: secreting a venom, to inject toxin**

"A murderer, that's who!" Josh answered, continuing to look through the contents of the briefcase, which proved to hold nothing more than what would be expected of a businessman. After securing the lock and leaving the case in its original place, Josh was distracted by a commotion from the closet. "Sydney, what are you doing in there?"

"I'm looking for the murder weapon!'

"Well, did you find anything?"

"There's a wooden box here. But it is sealed. It's labeled 'fragile.' And look over here, it says 'microscope and chemicals-handle with care.' Do you suppose this could be anything?"

"That dreadful book did have a chapter in it on how to make poisons that could not be detected," Josh said.

"Poison! Wait! I saw it …. It's in his hunting bag. I saw it!"

"What are you talking about, Sydney?"

Sydney   then wildly ***rummaged*** about Mr. Stevenson's things until she produced what she was looking for. "Look!" It was a plastic bag with a white powder. It was located at the bottom of his hunting bag. It was rat poison. "I didn't think anything of it at first. But, in light of the book we found, it could be a murder weapon. Right?"

• **Rummaged: search unsystematically and untidily through a mass or receptacle**

"I don't think rat poison is a part of standard hunting gear. I mean, I don't think Dad ever takes it with him when he goes hunting. I think you might be right."

"What should we do? Should we take it?" she asked.

"I think we have a responsibility to take it for Mr. Peterson's sake. Hurry, put everything back as it was. It's been almost fifteen minutes, so, we need to go!" Josh said, pointing to his watch.

As Mr. O'Neal searched Room 334, he was sure the large boots he had come across had to belong to Fred Moore. The signs of a skilled hunter were clearly there. He had not one rifle, but three. Going through his briefcase, he came across a letter from Mr. Peterson to Mr. Moore. It was apparently a letter of reprimand. Its undertones were somewhat harsh. Apparently, Mr. Moore had made a major decision affecting the company without consulting with Mr. Peterson. It seemed Mr. Moore had been placed on probation. His job was on the line. The letter was dated six months earlier. That's strange, thought Jake O'Neal, that's when the threats began on Peterson's life. Was it a coincidence? Or was it motive?

"Sydney, you look ghostly. You are so pale. Did something happen?" Mr. O'Neal asked his daughter.

"Oh Dad! I think we may have found the murder weapon!"

"Yeah, Dad. We know who the killer is! It's Mr. Stevenson!" Josh added.

"That's what you said about Bill Clark. Now come on. We've got to get going. The meeting will be breaking up soon."

"But Dad, we haven't finished searching the rooms," Josh said.

"We'll have to do that later. Let's go take in some scenery and compare notes."

"I'm for that. I think I can use a little fresh air," Sydney said, regaining some of her color and composure.

Chapter 7 Definitions Review

1. **Exuberantly: filled with a lively energy and excitement**
2. **Epitome: a person or thing that is a perfect example of a particular quality or type**
3. **Venomous: secreting a venom, to inject toxin**
4. **Rummaged: search unsystematically and untidily through a mass or receptacle**

Chapter 8

Sorting Clues on the Slippery Slopes

The gentlemen were just *adjourning* their unscheduled meeting when the three O'Neals, with ski gear in hand, arrived in the lobby, ready to depart the lodge. "I wish I were going with you," the youngest of the gentlemen said, as they crossed paths.

"Guys, this is Bill Clark. Bill, my two kids, Josh and Sydney."

"Hi," the kids said, somewhat cautiously, remembering his intrusion into room 331 earlier.

"Is there something wrong?" Bill asked, noticing Josh was studying his shoes. "Uh, no... I just. uh. I think your shoes are cool," Josh said, embarrassed at being so *conspicuous*.

"Don't mind him. He's into shoes. He wants to be a shoe salesman," Sydney said, trying to cover for him.

"I hope they meet with your approval," he said, with a very *congenial* smile.

- **Adjourning: break off a meeting with the intention of resuming it later**
- **Conspicuous: standing out to be clearly visible**
- **Congenial: pleasant because of a personality, qualities, or interests that are similar to one's own**

Josh shifted about awkwardly, grateful for the interruption by his father, as he introduced his children to the other gentlemen. He wanted to make sure his kids knew who everyone was. When he introduced Mr. Stevenson to them, Sydney went pale at the mention of his name. Her knees weakening, she leaned against her father for support.

"Are you okay, child?" Mr. Stevenson asked, reaching out to

offer his hand. "No! Don't touch me!" she said, drawing away from him, startling Mr. Stevenson. Then composing herself she said, "I'm alright really. It's just the *altitude*. I just got a little dizzy, that's all. Thank you, sir, but I'm alright, really."

After the introductions were complete, Mr. O'Neal and his two children left the lodge for their *excursion*, leaving the gentlemen to continue their morning agenda at the lodge. The morning was still young. The bright sun shone on the glistening white slopes. The air was very dry, yet cold beating on their wind scorched faces as they trekked their way up the slopes. The walk did them good. The freedom the outdoors offered allowed the kids to clear their heads and shake their fears. Once at the top they were ready to rehash the morning's findings with a clear head.

- **Altitude: the height of an object or point in relation to sea level or ground level**
- **Excursion: a short journey or trip**

"Now, what makes you think that Thomas Stevenson is a killer?"

"Look, Dad! We found rat poison in his room!" Sydney said, pulling the evidence out of her pocket.

Disappointed with the lack of response from his father, Josh offered a theory. "Well, don't you see? He is going to poison Mr. Peterson. And everyone will think it is a heart attack. You know he is not the most physically fit person. In this altitude, it would not be unusual for an old man to have a heart attack. It's the perfect crime."

"And, he has that very book in his room!" Sydney added.

"What book?" Mr. O'Neal asked.

"The Perfect Crime!" Sydney exclaimed. "And, what an evil looking book it is!" "Did you see anything else?" Mr. O'Neal asked.

"There was a wooden box containing a microscope and chemicals," Sydney added.

"You need to remember these gentlemen are from a pharmaceutical company. They may be working on some experiments. Chemicals, even rat poison, may not be so unusual. Nevertheless, it wouldn't hurt to be cautious around all of them."

"Dad, what was it you were looking for in Mr. Young's room?" Josh asked.

"It was a flyer advertising the Lost Lodge. He was the one who chose this particular spot for this weekend's meeting. A man who doesn't hunt or ski. I want to know why!"

"I noticed that he didn't have a rifle. But Dad, I saw a revolver in his room," Josh added.

"So did I," Jake O'Neal said, rubbing his chin, recalling what he had heard earlier. Young is 'anti-gun.' Why would someone who was so against guns have one in his room, he thought.

"Then maybe he is the killer," Sydney said.

"Let me make one thing clear. There is no killer. Not yet, anyway. We only have a threat on a life. Now, enough of this talk of murder. Let's have a little fun!" Mr. O'Neal said. "I'll race you two down the slope."

The three went gracefully up and down the slopes for the remainder of the morning and into the early afternoon. Their skiing was interrupted only by an occasional snowball fight that was usually *instigated* by Mr. O'Neal. He really loved his two children and enjoyed interacting with them. He was strong, and he could throw a mean snowball, but his two kids were clever. Sydney would *feign* some disaster, like a sprained ankle, causing her dad to come running to her aid. Josh would then catch him off guard and ambush him with a massive snowball. Then, together they would gang up on him, burying him in the snow. He fell for it every time. They laughed and played like the free spirits they were, enjoying the beautiful glow of the sun on the shimmering slopes.

- **Instigate: bring about or initiate**
- **Feign: pretend to be affected by**

Chapter 8 Definitions Review

1. **Adjourning:** break off a meeting with the intention of resuming it later
2. **Conspicuous:** standing out to be clearly visible
3. **Congenial:** pleasant because of a personality, qualities, or interests that are similar to one's own
4. **Altitude:** the height of an object or point in relation to sea level or ground level
5. **Excursion:** a short journey or trip
6. **Instigate:** bring about or initiate
7. **Feign:** pretend to be affected by

Chapter 9

Preparing for the Hunt

Later that afternoon, Jake O'Neal knocked at his children's door. They hadn't been back for more than an hour when the unwelcome knock came. They had eaten, showered, and were now ready for a nap, tired out by the day's excursion.

"Guys, I'm taking both of you deer hunting with me. I made a date with Mr. Peterson and a couple of his associates for four o'clock sharp.

"Oh boy!" said Josh excitedly.

"Well, Josh, I figured you would like the idea. And I know, Sydney, you're not much for hunting but bring your camera. The scenery is beautiful," he said, trying to encourage his daughter. "Go ahead, dress warmly. The temperature is dropping. I'll be waiting out here in the hall." He then proceeded to Mr. Peterson's room. After several knocks on the door, there was no answer. He then tried the door to see if it was open. It was locked.

"Peterson, are you in there?" Jake O'Neal shouted.

"Why, I am right here," a voice from behind said.

Jake O'Neal turned around to see Mr. Peterson coming out of room 333. He observed him locking the door behind him and placing the key in his pocket. "I thought you were staying in 331," Jake said, surprised.

"I was, but Bill asked if we could change rooms. He said something about the windows in his room would not open, and he likes to sleep with open windows. Quite frankly, I'm glad to be in a room where the widows remain shut."

"I wish you would have checked this out with me first," Jake said sternly. "It could be a setup."

"No way! Bill is a good ole boy. I don't think he is a suspect. Do you?" Charles Peterson asked nervously.

"I don't know what to think. Just the same, before you make any more changes, consult with me."

They were soon joined by Fred Moore, Thomas Stevenson, Scott McCauley, and Paul Pierce. All the men were dressed in well-worn hunting **attire** and equipped with hunting gear. Trailing behind was Sydney. As the men gathered, Mr. Peterson stood out being dressed in obviously new camouflage **apparel**.

- **Attire: clothes, especially fine or formal**
- **Apparel: clothing**

"Well, looky here. It's Indiana Jones. No, it's only Peterson," Fred Moore teased. "The way that hat falls over your eyes, be careful you don't shoot one of us."

"Let's be on our way. The mule deer are waiting," Mr. Peterson said enthusiastically.

"Aren't we going to wait for Bill?" Jake asked.

"He probably decided to go skiing. He'll turn up later, you'll see," Mr. Peterson said confidently.

"He sure sounded like he wanted to go on the hunt when we spoke of it at lunch," Fred Moore said. "Maybe he is in the shower." He then knocked on the door loudly.

"Clark! Are you in there?" Again, no answer came from the room.

"What's all the racket out here?" Carl Young said, sticking his head out of his room directly across the hallway.

"We're ready to go on the hunt. Would you like to come?" Stevenson taunted, knowing how he detested hunting. "By the way, have you seen Bill?"

"Yes, I saw him going downstairs about thirty minutes ago," Young said, yawning and rubbing his large belly. "Now, hold down the noise out here. I'm going to take a nap before supper. You know, on second thought, I distinctly remember Bill saying that he was going skiing." Then he turned to go into his room.

"There, now you have it. The mule deer are waiting. Let's go!"

Peterson said. They all departed, Peterson leading the way. He was like a child with a new toy. He was obviously a man who enjoyed a good hunt. The gleam had returned to his dull eyes.

Chapter 9 Definition Review

1. **Attire: clothes, especially fine or formal**
2. **Apparel: clothing**

Chapter 10

The Hunt

"We'd better hurry if we're going to do any hunting. It looks like the weather is going to get bad real soon," Peterson said.

"I think you are right," Fred Moore responded.

"This looks like a good place for deer. O'Neal, why don't you and your kids walk down to that ridge where you can watch that opening below. We'll walk back along the edge of the *ravine* where it is thick. I'll see if I can run a deer or two out by you," Peterson suggested.

• **Ravine: a deep, narrow gorge with steep sides**

"That sounds good. But why don't you let me go up there. It looks pretty steep," Jake said.

"No, no! I insist!" Peterson said.

Consenting to the suggestion, Jake O'Neal and the kids searched for a place to wait for the deer. As the five men climbed upward near the cliff, the O'Neals made their way down the slope. Finding a snow-covered log nestled between bushes, Mr. O'Neal brushed it off and took a seat with his kids.

"Don't make a sound, but get your camera ready, Sydney. It's a beautiful sight when the deer come running out of the thicket," her dad said.

"Dad, you're not going to shoot them, are you?" Sydney asked, her gray-green eyes pleading.

"No, I'm not going to shoot them, but Josh probably will," he said as he handed the rifle over to his son. "I tell you what, he won't shoot the first one. I'll save that one for you to snap a picture. But

I can't promise anything after that. If Josh doesn't shoot them, Fred Moore will. I'm sure of that."

Occasional yells came from the thicket as the men tried to scare the deer out of the brush. The three O'Neals waited in anticipation for the rush of deer. Sydney had her camera primed for the event, and Josh held the rifle tightly in anticipation of an upcoming shot. The atmosphere was still. All was quiet, then suddenly a loud, shrill scream filled the air.

"What was that?!" Josh asked.

"It's a cry for help! It's coming from the thicket," Jake O'Neal said, rising to his feet. "Come on and stay close to me."

"Don't worry. We'll stick to you like glue," Sydney pledged, gathering her camera supplies.

They quickly worked their way around the thicket and up next to the cliff's edge. They could hear brush breaking and the excited voices of the men somewhere in the distance. Following the voices, they soon came to the place where three of the men were gathered, peering over the cliff in unbelief.

"What happened?" Jake asked.

"He ... he fell off the cliff?!" Paul Pierce said excitedly, wringing his hunting cap in his hands.

The Lost Lodge

"Who!? Who fell off the cliff?" Jake insisted.

"It's Peterson. I heard him cry for help. But by the time I got here, it was too late. He must have slipped," Thomas Stevenson said.

Scott McCauley was in agreement with Stevenson's testimony. He also recognized the cry for help as coming from Charles Peterson. "It was definitely Peterson's voice," he said.

As Jake peered over the cliff into the deep, ragged ravine, he got a birds-eye view of the lifeless body of the man, lying far below on the snow-covered rocks. He couldn't help but feel some responsibility. He was hired to protect Peterson and flush out the killer. Now, he could only do the latter.

"Is it Mr. Peterson, Dad?" Josh whispered.

"I'm afraid so. It looks like Peterson alright." He then bent to the ground and retrieved the Indiana Jones hat that Charles Peterson had been wearing. It was sitting right at the cliffs edge where his body had obviously fallen over the edge.

"Could he still be alive?" Sydney asked.

"No, I think that would be impossible. Calculating the height from which he fell onto the rocks, the impact would cause a *lethal* blow. Did anyone see him fall?" Jake O'Neal asked.

• **Lethal: sufficient to cause death**

"No, we were all scattered out in the thicket," Scott McCauley said.

"I was on the other side of McCauley. I followed him up here when I heard the scream," Paul Pierce said.

"I followed Pierce," Thomas Stevenson said. "When we got here, we saw Peterson lying at the bottom of the ravine, just as he is now. There's no way to get down there to his body. Someone will have to get to him on horseback."

Sydney pulled her camera out and bent forward over the cliffs edge to take pictures. "Sydney, be careful you don't fall in yourself," Josh warned, pulling on her ski jacket to balance her. "What are you doing anyway?"

"I'm taking pictures for evidence. You really don't think he fell in, do you?" Sydney whispered.

"Of course not! Someone pushed him. But, who?" Josh whispered back to her.

Bang! A loud gunshot rang out, startling everyone. Josh instinctively ducked and released his grip on Sydney. Sydney jumped at the loud sound, and after losing the counterbalance provided by Josh, began slipping off the cliff's edge.

At the sound of the gunshot Jake glanced over at Josh just in time to see him releasing Sydney. Jake's gaze moved swiftly from Josh to Sydney as she began to lose balance and slip. He felt his heart skip a beat. Time seemed to stop around him. His daughter was slipping off the cliff about to meet the same fate as Mr. Peterson, but Jake O'Neal was frozen in place.

What felt like an eternity was only a matter of a fraction of a second. Jake snapped back to reality and plunged forward, managing to catch the hood of Sydney's jacket just as she was going over. He had a good grip on the jacket but feared Sydney would slip right out of it. Another gunshot rang out from further down the slope.

"Reach for my hand, Sydney!" he yelled. Sydney reached up with one hand and grabbed her dad's hand. "Give me your other hand, Sydney."

"I can't," Sydney said.

"Why not?" Jake O'Neal asked, trying to pull his daughter up.

"It's my camera. It's caught on a branch," Sydney said, pulling on the camera's strap.

"Let it go, Sydney. We can always get a new camera. I need to pull you up now before we both fall off this cliff."

"But Dad, I've almost got it loose," Sydney said, continuing to struggle for the freedom of her camera with one hand and hanging on to her life with the other.

"Sydney! Let it go! That's an order!" her dad said sternly.

"Just a second more and I'll have it! I promise."

Before he could protest again, he began to slip, the snow melting under him from his body heat.

The Lost Lodge

"Somebody! Help him!" Josh screamed.

The three men rose to the call like soldiers obeying the general's command. Mr. Pierce grabbed Jake's left leg while Mr. McCauley held onto the right leg, and Mr. Stevenson grabbed at his belt. Working together they pulled Jake, Sydney, and her camera to safety. Once up and away from the cliff's edge, Jake O'Neal embraced his daughter before thoroughly reprimanding her for her carelessness and stubbornness in not *relinquishing* her camera in view of their safety.

> - **Relinquishing: voluntarily cease to keep or claim, give up**

"I'm sorry, Dad. It was the gunshot. It startled me. That's all! I couldn't let go of my camera. I got some great shots."

"Well, I certainly hope it was worth it," Mr. O'Neal said exasperatedly.

"The gunshot!" Josh reminded them.

"It was coming from down the slope," Thomas Stevenson said, leading the group to where the shot was heard. Fred Moore was there, swearing at his rifle.

"What is it?" Paul Pierce demanded an explanation.

"My deer got away! I don't understand it," Moore said, continuing to swear.

"There's no need for you to use that kind of language, especially around my kids. You're here hunting. Haven't you been aware of anything going on here?" Jake asked.

"What's he talking about?" Moore asked, looking perplexed.

> - **Perplexed: of something complicated or unaccountable, causing someone to feel completely baffled**

"Peterson fell off the cliff. He's dead," Paul Pierce said, distressed over the whole matter.

"When my mind is set to kill deer, I block out everything else. I'm sorry about Peterson, but you know he wasn't in the best shape. He shouldn't have been climbing those hills like some young man. He probably couldn't see where he was going, wearing that ridiculous hat," Fred Moore said coldly.

"We'd better make our way back to the Lodge," McCauley said. "The snow is beginning to fall pretty heavily."

"I thought you always got your deer! So, what happened?" Stevenson taunted Moore, as they headed for the lodge.

"I don't understand! I know I got a good aim on him. No way could I have missed him! I shot, and the deer ... he just looked at me. Then he ran away! My scope must be off," Moore said, justifying his failure.

"Just admit it. You missed!" Stevenson said.

"I'm glad he got away," Sydney said softly.

Once at the Lodge, they reported to Mr. Roberts, the clerk, the events that occurred on the slopes.

"As soon as we can, we'll have to contact the sheriff's office so they can send someone to pick up the body," Mr. Roberts said.

"Why don't you contact them now?" Jake asked.

"The radio won't do us much good. There is too much static with the front that is moving in," Mr. Roberts explained.

"If we can't reach them by radio, can't you send Joe Strange to town for help?"

"Well, I would if I could. But I can't," Mr. Roberts said.

"What is that supposed to mean?" Jake asked, annoyed at the comment.

"It seems Mr. Strange has disappeared. He is not to be found," Roberts explained.

"Can't someone else drive the snowmobile?" Josh suggested.

"Now, there's another *dilemma*. I tried to start the snowmobile but to no avail. It seems the distributor has been removed. And we don't have a replacement."

- **Dilemma: situation in which difficult choices have to be made between two or more alternatives**

"Why would anyone want to sabotage the snowmobile?" Sydney asked. "Unless ...."

"Unless, someone doesn't want us leaving," Josh finished her sentence.

Mr. O'Neal looked at the unsuspecting group around the fire. Mr. Peterson had been murdered. No one knew that except he and the murderer. The others thought it to be merely an accident. It could have been any one of them. And what about Bill Clark? Could he have been waiting in the thicket for Mr. Peterson? Where was he?

"Dad, I want to go to my room to download my pictures," Sydney said.

Jake O'Neal saw the kids to their room, making sure of their safety. "I'll be back at seven sharp to take you to dinner." He then walked up and down the halls looking for anything out of the ordinary. As he approached Carl Young's room, he noticed the carpet seemed wet at the threshold, so he bent down to check. He had to have gone out in the snow for the carpet to be this wet. Just then the door swung open.

"Looking for something, O'Neal?" Carl Young asked.

"I dropped my keys. That's all." He then stood up, throwing his keys in the air, and catching them in mid-air. "Uh. I don't suppose you heard what happened today?"

"I'd wager a bet that someone killed a deer," Young said.

Jake O'Neal then filled him in on what happened to Mr. Peterson, watching his facial expressions closely for any trace of surprise or guilt, but there was neither. His countenance remained flat.

"Well, that's too bad," Mr. Young said.

Looking down at his pants, Mr. O'Neal noticed that Carl Young's pants and shoes were still damp. "Have you been outside?"

"Well, to tell you the truth, I couldn't sleep, after all the noise you all made in the hall this afternoon. So, I decided to join you. But

I got lost and came back the first chance I got."

Jake O'Neal studied him. He seemed a little uncomfortable at his last statement, like he wasn't totally being truthful. The conversation finished, and Jake returned to his room.

Chapter 10 Definition Review

1. **Ravine: a deep, narrow gorge with steep sides**
2. **Lethal: sufficient to cause death**
3. **Relinquishing: voluntarily cease to keep or claim, give up**
4. **Perplexed: of something complicated or unaccountable, causing someone to feel completely baffled**
5. **Dilemma: situation in which difficult choices have to be made between two or more alternatives**

Chapter 11

Who Ordered the Tea?

It was seven sharp and most of the guests had taken their places at the dinner tables as Sarah began to bring out her *delectable* dishes. Of course, Mr. Peterson's chair was empty. But so was Bill Clark's.

"Has anyone seen Bill?" Jake O'Neal asked.

"Not since early this afternoon," Mr. Young said. "As I told you earlier."

"Don't you think we should go look for him?" Jake asked.

"You go. I'm *famished*. We can't let this good food get cold," Mr. Young said, grabbing the hot rolls Sarah had just set before them.

- **Delectable: delicious**
- **Famished: extremely hungry**

"Yes, Bill can take care of himself. He's a young man, unlike the rest of us," Fred Moore said bitterly.

"Well, all the same, I'm going to look for him," Jake said. "Kids, you come with me."

"I'm going with you, too" Scott McCauley said.

"So am I," Paul Pierce said, following after them.

There was no answer to the loud knocks on Bill Clark's door. The door was locked. They had asked Mr. Roberts for a key, but he had refused. He said it would be an invasion of his privacy and that there was no just cause to break in.

"I think we should break the door down," Paul Pierce suggested. "Move aside!" He then moved as far away from the door as possible to give him some running room. He plowed his shoulders into the door and bounced off it like a rubber ball.

"Are you hurt?" Jake asked, lending him a hand.

"No, only my pride," Paul Pierce said, rubbing his shoulder.

"Let me try," Jake said. He threw his weight back onto one leg, then hurled his weight back into the door with the other leg, kick-style motion, forcing the door open. A horrified gasp came from the kids as the door flung open to reveal the body of Bill Clark, lying prone on the floor. Jake walked over to the body, knelt beside it, and felt for a pulse. Bill Clark's color was ashen. There were no *obvious* signs of *trauma*. "His body is cold, and he's beginning to stiffen. He's probably been dead for about three or four hours. There's nothing we can do. We'll have to wait for the sheriff. Perhaps an autopsy can be done tomorrow. Do any of you know if he had been sick?"

- **Obvious: easily perceived or understood, clear**
- **Trauma: injury to the body, deeply distressing or disturbing experience**

"No, he was the picture of health. He exercised regularly," Scott McCauley answered.

"Something fishy is going on around here. First Peterson, and now Bill! Both are dead!" Paul Pierce said in disbelief. "This is just too strange!"

Jake searched the room for clues. It appeared Bill Clark drank something shortly before he died. The glass was on the floor beside him. Picking up the cup with a handkerchief, he could see there were still a few drops of the beverage left in the glass. It was odorless and looked something like tea. "Josh bring me Sydney's camera, and I will take some pictures of the body, before we move it. Scott and Paul, are you guys equipped to do a drug screen?" Jake asked.

"What are you getting at, Jake? Do you think Bill could have been poisoned?" Scott McCauley asked.

"You think he was murdered!?" Paul Pierce asked again in disbelief.

"It's possible. Did Bill have any enemies?" Jake asked.

"Are you *insinuating* one of us did it?" Paul Pierce asked.

pacing up and down, wringing his hands together.

- **Insinuating: suggest or hint**

"We've been together for years. I can assure you, there is not a murderer among us. Moore and Stevenson used to give Bill a hard time. Maybe we all did. But it was just because he was so much younger than the rest of us. Peterson used to say that Bill would probably be the one to take his place when he retired. That really made us mad, seeing we have been with the company a lot longer than Bill," McCauley added.

"Did Peterson have enemies?" Jake asked.

"Now what? You think he was murdered too?" Pierce asked, throwing his hands up in the air.

"For Pete's sake! He fell off the cliff," Scott McCauley said.

"Did you actually see him fall?" Josh interrupted.

"Yeah, did anyone see him fall?" Sydney echoed.

"Let me handle this," Jake O'Neal said, motioning his kids to get behind him.

"No, we didn't. We just assumed that ... he fell," Paul Pierce said thoughtfully.

"I have to admit, none of us liked him. He was not a very likeable man. He was always driving everyone. His secretary said he used to be a pleasant man, until his son died some fifteen years ago. He's never been the same since. But none of us disliked him enough to kill him. No, I think it was an accident. It had to be," Scott McCauley said.

"If they were murdered ..." Paul Pierce's anxiety was mounting. "We're stuck in this God-forsaken igloo out in the middle of nowhere. We have no communication with the outside world, and a murderer is among us. How do we know that you're not the murderer, O'Neal? Who are you anyway? And why are you always sticking your big nose into everyone's business?"

"My dad is not a murderer!" Josh exclaimed, coming to his

father's defense.

"Yeah, he's one of the good guys!" Sydney added.

"Guys, I told you, I will handle this," Jake said.

"One of the good guys?" Josh mocked Sydney. "What do you think this is, 'cops' and 'robbers'? Give me a break!"

"Of course ... it could be someone who works here. What ever happened to that Joe Strange fellow? If you ask me, he was pretty strange alright," Paul Pierce said.

"And what about Mr. Roberts, the clerk? He is such a cold man. He gives me the creeps," Scott McCauley added.

"First things first, men. How long will it take you two to do a drug screen?"

"About an hour if it is a common drug, maybe longer," McCauley answered.

Jake took numerous pictures of the body and room. He then went over to Bill Clark's body, picked him up and gently placed him on the bed, folding his hands across his chest. He had a peaceful look on his face, as if he were sleeping.

Josh looked at the still body. "Dad, this was supposed to be Mr. Peterson's room. Do you think the murderer made a mistake and killed Bill Clark by accident? Look at him. He looks so peaceful. And you know Sydney thought he was so cute."

"I think you're right," Jake said.

"You thought he was cute, too?" Josh asked.

"No! I think you are right about the killer making a mistake. I think he made a big mistake. Now, let's return to our rooms. Keep your doors locked. We will all meet down in the diner in an hour and see if we can figure this all out. I'll tell the others," Jake instructed as he escorted his children to their room. "Sydney, did you develop those pictures yet?"

"They are not finished yet, why?"

"Can you blow up the shots you took of Peterson's body?"

"Sure, but why?"

"Just maybe, if you took the right shot, I can prove if Peterson was indeed murdered or not. Can you have it ready in an hour?"

"I'll get on it right away."

The Lost Lodge

"I'm going to look around some more. Joshua, you stay here with Sydney and keep your door locked. That's an order. I'll be back for you in about an hour. Stay out of trouble."

Chapter 11 Definitions Review

1. **Delectable: delicious**
2. **Famished: extremely hungry**
3. **Obvious: easily perceived or understood, clear**
4. **Trauma: injury to the body, deeply distressing or disturbing experience**
5. **Insinuating: suggest or hint**

Chapter 12

The Missing Snowmobile

Sydney moved quickly to assemble her 'darkroom' in the bathroom. She had become *fascinated* with photography and was getting pretty good at it. She had learned much about photography from her late mother, who always loved to take pictures of her family.

"Help me with this chair, Josh."

"What do you need the chair for?"

"I'm going to put it against the door. This place is spooky. The only thing that can make it worse is if the lights were to go out." Almost on key, the lights began to flicker, and then all went dark.

"Now you did it!" Josh said.

"What did I do?" Sydney asked.

"Everything is pitch black. I can't even see my own hand. Or is that your hand?" Josh asked, fumbling in the dark.

"It's my hand! Now quit messing around and help me find the bathroom. My lights for the darkroom are battery operated. We don't need a lot of light anyway. The pictures will turn out great! Let's hurry, we don't have much time."

Meanwhile, Jake O'Neal had made his way down the dark hallway to the second floor. Wearing his infra-red glasses he had brought along, he could see to some extent in the dark. Cautiously, he picked the lock and made his way down the darkened *corridor* to where he had seen the blonde woman the night before. He could hear voices coming from one of the rooms.

- **Fascinated: draw the irresistibly attention and interest**
- **Corridor: long passage in a building where doors lead to rooms**

Following the voices he came to a closed door, knelt on one knee and peered through the keyhole. He could see the woman sitting at a table, the candlelight burning brightly. She was talking to a man. Though he could not see his face, he recognized the man by his bright yellow overcoat and the red disheveled hair that was partially covered by a fire-engine red cap. It was Joe Strange. His voice was low and familiar, yet there was no *detection* of that hillbilly slang that characterized Joe Strange. Was it all an act? Who was the man, really? Who was this woman? Were they hired to kill Mr. Peterson? His thoughts were interrupted by the turn of a key at the stairwell door. Jake swiftly retreated into the shadows. He could see a flash of light under the doorway. Then, the creaking of the door opening could be heard, followed by slow deliberate footsteps. He could not see who it was. Not wanting to risk being found out, he stayed very quiet in the shadows. The man knocked on the door where the woman and Joe Strange were.

- **Detection: process of identifying something that is concealed**

"Who is it?" The woman asked.

"It is I, Mrs. White, Jonathan Roberts. May I come in?" He said in his formal, staunch manner.

"What is it, Jonathan? And why are the lights out?" The woman asked. Her voice was rough and demanding.

"It's that Mr. O'Neal, Madam. He is asking far too many questions. And as far as the lights are concerned, I believe it to be a burnt fuse. I am locating one now."

"Don't worry about O'Neal. He doesn't know anything. Take him to Joe's room.

Let him do a little snooping there. I think that will solve our problem."

"Very well, Madam, as you say. I have Mr. White's cocktail. May I bring it in to him?"

The Lost Lodge

"Okay, but make it fast, Jonathan. I don't like the dark. I want you to get the lights on as soon as possible. And when is my shower going to be fixed? I am tired of sneaking upstairs for my shower. Did anyone see you coming up here?"

"No, Madam. No one saw me. And as far as the shower goes, I'm afraid that will just have to wait." Mr. Roberts' voice was fading. He had apparently gone into the room to see Mr. White. "Here is your cocktail, sir. I made it myself."

Jake had to really concentrate to hear what was being said now. The voices were low and distant. They were all inside the room now. He dare not come out of the shadows until Mr. Roberts was gone.

"Jonathan, you are really playing the part well. I have to hand it to you," the familiar male's voice said from inside the room.

"Well, we have rehearsed it enough. Haven't we, my dear Mr. White."

"Yes, we have. We've finally come in for the kill! Now, take care of that meddlesome O'Neal, before he spoils everything."

Jake was trying to put the pieces together. Mr. White was the owner of the Lodge. The blonde woman was evidently his wife. Were Joe Strange and Mr. White indeed one and the same? Mrs. White had been sneaking upstairs for showers. That would explain the strands of hair Josh found in Mr. Peterson's room, and also the missing bath towels.

Could Joe Strange have actually been the missing caretaker, as was told in the legend? Was he the owner of the Lodge? Where was Joe Strange's southern *dialect* now? Was it all an act? Who was Joe Strange, and what was his relation to Mr. Peterson? Why would he want to kill Bill Clark? Did he plan to kill us all? He suddenly thought of his kids. I need to get them out of here, he thought, and now. He waited eagerly for Mr. Roberts' departure. Assured that he was gone, Jake escaped the second floor without notice. He went to the dining room and filled Thomas Stevenson, Fred Moore, and Carl Young in on what had happened to Bill Clark. But he didn't mention anything about what he had encountered on the second floor. He didn't know yet who was to be trusted. He only wanted to get his children to safety before anything else happened.

"I want to get my children to town tonight, if possible," Jake informed the men.

"I'm going to see if the radio is working yet."

Mr. Roberts was at his usual place at the desk when Jake approached him.

"Is the radio working yet?" Jake asked.

"No, the storm is still causing too much interference. We will just have to weather the storm."

"Has Joe Strange returned yet?"

"No ... but, perhaps we can check his room. Would you like to accompany me,

Mr. O'Neal? I have a key."

"Wouldn't you consider that an invasion of privacy? Isn't that against your policy?" Jake said *sarcastically*.

- **Dialect: a particular form of language which is peculiar to a specific region or social group**
- **Sarcastically: use of irony to mock or convey contempt**

"In light of today's events, I think I can make an exception. His room is right down the hall. Follow me. I see you have a flashlight. How convenient," Mr. Roberts said, with a tinge of suspicion in his voice.

"I was in my room when the lights went out. I had a flashlight with me. Every prepared hunter carries one, you know."

Jake O'Neal followed Mr. Roberts very cautiously, remembering what he had heard a few minutes earlier. Mr. Roberts knocked on the door several times. There was no answer. Mr. Roberts then inserted the key into the door and began to push.

"It seems to be stuck. I can't get it to open. Perhaps you can try, young man," Mr.Roberts said, then moved far away from the door.

Jake stepped to the side of the doorway, reached his hand over the doorknob, turned it slowly, and pushed it with a jolt. Blam! The door shattered from shotgun blast from inside the room, barely missing Jake.

"Oh, my goodness!" Mr. Roberts exclaimed. "We could have been blasted to smithereens if we had been standing in front of the door. However, did you know, my good man?"

"Just a hunch," Jake said, peering through the doorway. "It was a booby trap. The shotgun had a string running from the trigger to the door where it was looped over the doorknob. As the door was pushed open, it tightened the string, pulling the trigger, causing it to discharge."

Just moments after the shotgun blast the three executives, who had been in the dining room, appeared at the scene. Fred Moore and Thomas Stevenson had their rifles in hand. Carl Young cowered behind them.

"What happened?" Fred Moore asked, holding his rifle in ready position.

"It appears Joe Strange didn't want any company," Jake answered.

"Why would Joe Strange do such a *horrid* thing? We could have been killed!" Mr. Roberts exclaimed.

- **Horrid: such as to cause horror, shockingly dreadful**

"Maybe he had something to hide," Jake said, entering the room. "You all wait out here until I see if it is safe."

There were pictures of Joe, a woman, and two small children on his dresser. On the back of the picture, the names 'Joe, Jane, Jimmy, and Kit' were written. This must be the family he lost in the hurricane, Jake thought. Or was he indeed from Alabama at all? He wasn't sure of anything at the moment. Empty boxes of gun shells, an empty gun case, and several hunting magazines were sprawled about the floor. The *paraphernalia* on the small desk in the corner caught his eye. It was cuttings from newspaper, scissors, glue, and plain paper. It could have been the makings of the threatening letter that Mr. Peterson had received. What was the connection between

Peterson, Robert White, and Joe Strange? Why Bill Clark?

"Well, is it safe to come in now?" Fred Moore asked impatiently.

Jake quickly picked up the newspaper clippings and hid it in his jacket. He would have to examine it more closely later. "It's safe! You can come in now," he called out. Stevenson stood in awe, with his mouth hanging open. "Whoever set this trap knew exactly what he was doing."

"What do you mean, whoever? I think it is clear enough. Joe Strange murdered Peterson, Clark, and almost blew up Roberts and O'Neal here. I think we got a psycho on our hands. What do you think, O'Neal? You're supposed to know the criminal mind," Carl Young said, breathing rapidly, obviously short of breath.

Jake looked vigilantly at the four men before him. He wasn't sure of any of them. There was no one he could trust just yet. He couldn't help but think that someone with Brexler Laboratories was involved. But who? Ignoring Carl Young's question, he turned to Mr. Roberts. "Was Joe much of a hunter?"

- **Paraphernalia: miscellaneous articles**
- **Vigilantly: keenly watchful to detect danger; wary**

"He did partake of the sport on occasion," Mr. Roberts answered.

"His gun is missing, and he obviously took a lot of ammunition with him. His belongings are still here. It looks as though he had plans to return," Jake said.

"One thing is for sure. He wasn't the cleanest man, by any means," Mr. Roberts said, passing his hand over the dresser, then blowing the dust into air.

"This thing is getting a bit out of control. I need to get my kids to safety. Is there any other means of transportation?"

"Well, there are two small snowmobiles. But they are of no consequence. They are two-seaters and not made for travel. We use them for fun or to run nearby errands."

"Can you take me to them?" Jake asked.

The Lost Lodge

"I want to get out of here too," Carl Young said. "I'm going with you. Besides, you can only carry one passenger with you. I can take one of your kids."

The small group headed for the back garage, Mr. Roberts leading the way with a lantern. The winds were howling. A cutting chill was in the air, but the snow had lightened up. A halfmoon yielded enough light for them to see one another at close range. The darkness enhanced the brilliance of the stars. What a ***paradox*** God's creation held this evening. On one hand, nature shouted out the beauty of His imagination and creativity, while in the midst of this beauty lurked the very evil and wickedness of a murderer. How difficult it was to understand how good and evil could be in such close ***proximity***. Entering into the small garage, only one vehicle was to be seen.

- **Paradox: seemingly absurd or self-contradictory statement**
- **Proximity: nearness in space, or relationship**

"There's only one! Where is the other one?" Carl Young exclaimed.

"Did Joe Strange have a key?" Jake asked.

"Yes, he had a key," Mr. Roberts said.

"I guess we can assume Joe Strange made off with the snowmobile, that low life!" Young said, continuing to curse him under his breath.

Taking the key from Mr. Roberts, Jake climbed onto the remaining snowmobile.

"Wait, O'Neal. I'll give you five hundred dollars cash if you take me into town before your children," Young said, reaching for his wallet.

"You scumbag," Fred Moore shouted.

"Okay … okay ... make it a thousand dollars!" Young pleaded.

"No money in the world is worth more than my children's safety.

I will speak to the authorities and send help as soon as possible." He then put the key into the ignition, turned the key, while all looked on with anticipation. But nothing happened. He tried again and again. But it was useless. It was dead.

"What's wrong? Why won't it start? Do something!" Young said, his voice escalating.

Jake then proceeded to lift the hood to check the engine. Stevenson was looking over his shoulder.

"It's no mystery why it won't start. What a mess!" Thomas Stevenson said.

"The distributor and the spark plug wires have been removed. Even the battery cables have been cut in several places. Whoever *sabotaged* this vehicle did a very thorough job," Jake explained.

"Joe Strange, that's who!" Young said. "I've got to get out of here. If we stay here, we'll all be killed. Is there any other way we can get to town?"

"You can walk," Mr. Roberts said coldly.

"It's got to be at least twenty miles down the mountain. Few men would have the *stamina* to make a trek like that in the snow. It's late. I don't think that's an option," Jake said.

- **Sabotaged: deliberately destroy, damage**
- **Stamina: the ability to sustain prolonged physical or mental effort**

"What about the other snowmobile? Joe Strange must have it somewhere,"Moore said, stirring up some hope. "If we find it, we can take it by force. I say, let's hunt him down, before he hunts us down."

"Is there any other place Joe could have taken the snowmobile?" Jake asked.

"Why, we have always left them in the garage here. We have searched the grounds. It is not to be found," Mr. Roberts said, heading for the hotel.

The Lost Lodge

"Wait a minute, Roberts. Think, is there anywhere else Strange could have hidden the snowmobile?" Jake demanded.

"No! Absolutely not. He has disappeared, and apparently he's taken the snowmobile with him. We will have to wait for the weather to clear and for the authorities to settle the matter. Until then, I suggest you all go to your rooms and remain there!"

"There's a cabin about a mile from here. I saw it," Carl Young offered, biting on his bottom lip.

"A cabin?" Moore asked.

"Yes, I went for a walk this afternoon. I saw it then."

"Well, what about this cabin, Roberts?" Jake asked, waiting to see how he would explain away the cabin.

"Oh! That cabin. I nearly forgot about it. Thank you for reminding me. There is a two-room cabin with a fireplace, firewood, and basic essentials. It's used by hunters who may want to stay out all night. It is about a mile up the slope. That way," Mr. Roberts said, pointing out into the blackness of the night.

"I'll bet that's where he is. Did you see the snowmobile, Carl?" Moore asked.

"No, I didn't get that close. It could have been behind the cabin. Come to think of it, I think I saw smoke coming from the chimney. I didn't see much more. I got short winded going uphill. So, I turned around and went back to the hotel."

"I'm going after him. Are you with me, O'Neal?" Fred Moore asked.

"I think it's a good possibility the vehicle is there. Yes, I'm with you. I'm for retrieving the snowmobile," Jake agreed.

"What about you, Stevenson? You've been terribly quiet. Are you in?" Moore asked.

"No, I think I will stay at the Lodge. If you scare him away, he just may come here. I'll be ready for him," Stevenson said, cocking his rifle. His face was stone-like, his eyes dull and cold.

"I'll stay with Stevenson," Young said nervously.

Mr. O'Neal was not totally comfortable about leaving his kids at the Lodge. But he did want to get them to safety. He needed the snowmobile. He knew where Joe Strange was earlier, as he had seen him on the second floor. But could he **confide** in Fred Moore? Mr. Roberts was in on it somehow. He would surely let Joe Strange know about the plan to take over the snowmobile. They needed to be prepared for anything. The two men, dressed in camouflage clothing, each carrying a rifle, made their way up the tree line to where the forest thickened, and approached the area where they calculated the cabin to be.

"I like a good hunt, O'Neal. But I never thought I would be hunting a man," Moore said.

"Let's spread out a little and work our way up this ridge to the other side. If he is up there, we don't want to get in his view. He's armed and dangerous," Jake said.

As they moved through the thicket up the ridge they tried to be as quiet as possible, but with the brush this thick it was impossible to prevent the cracking of sticks and branches from echoing under their feet. The moon light shone **sporadically** through the cloud cover, almost as a spotlight over the **desolate** cabin. There were no lights on in the cabin. It appeared to be vacant. Jake slowly made his way to the back of the cabin. There it was. The snowmobile was under a small shelter. He climbed into the seat, inserted the key, and turned the ignition. But, just as before, nothing happened.

- **Confide: tell someone a secret or private matter**
- **Sporadic: occurring at different times, scattered**
- **Desolate: deserted of people and in a state of bleak**

"Not this one too?!" Moore exclaimed, joining Jake.

"I'm afraid so," Jake said, lifting the hood.

Just as before, the snowmobile had been sabotaged. Fred Moore decided to go around the cabin to look around. It had begun to snow pretty heavily again, making it difficult to see clearly more than a few feet ahead. Jake was looking around for some tools to see what he could do to get the snowmobile started, when he heard a rifle shot, and then another. He worked his way around the cabin, not knowing what he would find. Even with the snow falling, the moon was still able to shine brightly to the front of the cabin, as it peered through the sporadic cloud covering. Moore lay *supine* on the snow. It had to be him. No one had feet as big as Moore's. He quickly ran to where Moore was, pulled him out of the moonlight, and dragged him into the brush, leaving a trail of blood behind him. The *assailant* had disappeared. Groans were coming from Mr. Moore. He was still alive. He had been shot in the left shoulder. Jake quickly bandaged the wound using some of his own clothing.

- **Supine: lying face upward (as opposed to Prone which is lying face downward)**
- **Assailant: a person who physically attacks another**

"Are you okay?"

"Yes, he was probably aiming for my heart, but he got the shoulder."

"Did you see who it was?"

"Yes, it was Strange alright."

"Are you sure? It's hard to see with the snow falling."

"Positive! Who else is stupid enough to wear a red hat and a yellow jacket? It was him."

"I heard two shots. Did you shoot him?" Jake asked.

"I don't understand. I saw him aiming for me. It's as though he let me get in the first shot. I had a good aim on him, but I missed. Just like the deer. I should have killed that deer. I know I had him," Fred Moore insisted.

"The snow was falling pretty heavily. It would be hard to hit any target with this much snow and the poor lighting," Jake challenged.

"No, I had a good aim on him. I shouldn't have missed."

"Didn't you think that your scope was off?"

"But this is a different rifle. I changed it after the hunt. I brought three rifles on this trip."

Jake gathered some brush to make a gurney. He secured Fred Moore on it, then started back for the Lodge. The snow was steadily coming down, and the temperature was getting colder by the minute. Fred Moore had lost a lot of blood and was beginning to get weak. He was a strong man with a strong constitution. He wasn't complaining, but Jake knew that he had to be in a lot of pain. He was a fighter. Jake knew that time was of the *essence*.

Jake needed to get him back to the lodge to get some proper medical attention. If he could get him back to the lodge in a timely manner, he would be okay. He proceeded to drag him back to the hotel, making sure he stayed out of the moon's light. Wolves could be heard howling in the distance. If the wolves got hold of the scent of blood, he would have other *predators* to contend with. He prayed that wouldn't happen.

- **Essence: the indispensable quality of something**
- **Predators: animal that naturally preys on others**

Chapter 12 Definitions Review

1. **Fascinated: draw the irresistibly attention and interest**
2. **Corridor: long passage in a building where doors lead to rooms**
3. **Detection: process of identifying something that is concealed**
4. **Dialect: a particular form of language which is peculiar to a specific region or social group**
5. **Sarcastically: use of irony to mock or convey contempt**
6. **Horrid: such as to cause horror, shockingly dreadful**
7. **Paraphernalia: miscellaneous articles**
8. **Vigilantly: keenly watchful to detect danger; wary**
9. **Paradox: seemingly absurd or self-contradictory statement**
10. **Proximity: nearness in space, or relationship**
11. **Sabotaged: deliberately destroy, damage**
12. **Stamina: the ability to sustain prolonged physical or mental effort**
13. **Confide: tell someone a secret or private matter**
14. **sporadic: occurring at different times**
15. **Desolate: deserted of people and in a state of bleak**
16. **Supine: lying face upward (as opposed to Prone which is lying face downward)**
17. **Assailant: a person who physically attacks another**
18. **Essence: the indispensable quality of something**
19. **Predators: animal that naturally preys on others**

Chapter 13

A Long Trip Back to the Lodge

Making their way down the mountain, the trail became more difficult to see. Snow continued to fall, and the wind was picking up now. Jake began to feel the strain from pulling the weight of Fred Moore. They were going against the wind, adding to the weight. The wind beat bitterly upon his cheeks. He dared not use his flashlight lest he become a target for the killer, who lurked around. He was sure Joe Strange had headed back for the hotel, but would he lay in wait for the two of them first? Would he anticipate their course down to the Lodge? They continued to stay in the shadows, but it was getting more and more difficult to see.

"Are you okay, Moore? Moore! Did you hear me?"

"I … I'm so cold," he said with quivering lips. His entire body was shaking, and his lips were blue.

"Stay with me, Fred. Don't go to sleep! We don't have much farther to go."

Jake checked the wound. It had begun to bleed again. He tightened the bandage as best he could. He then took his outer goose-down jacket off and wrapped it around Moore. After encouraging his companion to stay awake and fight, he began to rise to *commence* his journey. But as he did, a cold chill went up Jake's spine. He knew someone was watching him. He could feel the eyes upon him. He knew his predator was nearby.

- **Commence: begin, start**

"Be very still," Jake said to Moore. "We're not alone."

"Go on without me. You're an easy target if you hang on to me. I'm only slowing you down."

"Be quiet! I'm going to reach for my rifle. Then I'm going to make my move." Jake was up on his feet in a second flat, ready to face his opponent.

It was what he expected. His eyes locked with the yellow, piercing eyes of a hungry wolf who caught the scent of flesh and blood. Jake knew that the wolf would fight him for Moore's body. He only had moments before the aggressor's call would bring in the rest of the pack to share in the meal. He had to move quickly and accurately. The Lodge was very near, but with the present obstacles, it seemed like miles away. He had to stay focused. With *precision* timing, he cocked his rifle, aimed, and fired. The wolf was only six feet away.

The Lost Lodge

How could I miss, Jake thought as the wolf jumped forward. Jake moved swiftly about the snow, but his opponent was swifter. The wolf sunk his teeth deep into his boot. Jake took the opportunity to hit the scavenger with a hard blow to the head with the butt of his rifle. The blow did not seem to slow him down. In fact, it enraged him, causing him to let go of the boot and attach himself to Jake's right arm. Jake moved painfully, continuing in the fight. Fred Moore tried to reach his gun, but he was much too weak. He lay there helpless. Jake threw his body forward onto the wolf, trying to use all his weight to fight the dangerous beast. The pain in his arm was almost unbearable. In spite of the agony, he kept up the struggle. If I could just free my right arm long enough to reach the knife in my pant leg, he thought, just maybe .... But he was losing strength, and the pain was breaking his concentration.

Then he remembered his children, Josh and Sydney. He recalled the pain they experienced when they lost their mother in an unexpected accident, just three years earlier. He couldn't put them through that pain again by losing this fight. With a new sense of mission and *adrenalin* flowing through his body, he rolled over onto his back, the viscous animal now on top of him. Then, with every ounce of strength he could muster, he picked himself up and threw all of his weight onto the wolf with a new resolve. The breath was knocked out of the hungry beast for just a moment, allowing Jake to reach for his knife, and with split-second timing, he thrust the sharp hunting knife deep into his *adversary's* throat. The wolf went limp. Jake fell to his knees, writhing in pain. His breath was deep and heavy. He felt the pain pierce his lungs as he breathed in the freezing air. The temperature continued to drop. They had to get going before the other wolves moved in. He had managed to overcome one, a scout, no doubt. But he knew he couldn't fight off a pack. He hurriedly bandaged his right arm with some of his clothing, then continued down the trail, dragging Fred Moore on the home-made gurney.

As they neared the Lodge, they heard voices.

"Moore! O'Neal! Is that you?" Stevenson called out, running out to meet the two wounded men. "What happened?"

"Moore's been shot. It may have been Joe Strange. Have you seen him?'

"No, we haven't seen a thing. Your arm is bleeding. Did you get shot too?"

"No, it was a wolf, but I'm okay. We need to get Moore by the fire. We've got to warm him up quickly. I've been dragging him in the snow. If we don't move fast, frostbite will set in. I'm sure he's already suffering from *hypothermia*."

- **Adrenalin: hormone secreted by adrenal glands that prepares muscles for exertion**
- **Adversary: one's opponent in a contest**
- **Hypothermia: abnormally low body temperature**

"I'll take care of Fred. You get yourself inside. You look like you've had enough exposure to the cold also. I'll get Sarah to put something warm on," Stevenson instructed.

Sarah came to the aid of the two injured men as soon as she heard there was a need. She brought in fresh bandages, liniment, warm beverages, and plenty of blankets. She warmed bricks in the fireplace, wrapped them in cloth   and placed them on the feet of both Moore and Jake. She was the self-appointed nurse who took control, feeling very comfortable in dishing out orders to anyone around.

"You," she said, looking at Mr. Roberts, "keep giving Mr. Moore sips of this broth until he warms up. And don't take no for an answer. Give it to him whether he wants it or not."

"But, Madam, I have work to do. I am not a nursemaid."

"No work is more important than nursing these folks back to health." Then looking at Stevenson, she said, "And you, I want you to massage the hands and feet of Mr. Moore here until they warm up and the feeling comes back into them."

Sarah worked quickly to clean and bandage the wounds of Fred and Jake. As soon as she had finished bandaging Jake, he stood up to leave.

"And just where do you think you are going, John Wayne?" Sarah asked, in army Sergeant style,

"I've got to check on my kids."

"You just sit yourself down before the fire and get warmed up. I'll send Roberts to check on them."

"No! No, really, I'm fine. I want to see my kids. I've been gone for some time now. They must be worried."

"You're not going anywhere until you drink this potion I made for you. It will warm you up," Sarah insisted.

Jake was feeling very fatigued, and the pain was intensifying. A fever had already begun to set in. He knew he would never get away from Sarah unless he consented to drink her remedy. The concoction he sipped on was *rejuvenating*. The bite of the bitter cold was beginning to lose its hold over him. His eyes became very heavy. He felt his body giving in to sleep against his will as the agonizing pain began to ease. He tried hard to fight it but to no avail.

He drifted off into deep slumber, in the oversized chair, welcoming the warmth of the fire.

- **Rejuvenating: make to look or feel younger, fresher, or more lively**

Chapter 13 Definitions Review

1. **Commence: begin, start**
2. **Precision: marked by exactness**
3. **Adrenalin: hormone secreted by adrenal glands that prepares muscles for exertion**
4. **Adversary: one's opponent in a contest**
5. **Hypothermia: abnormally low body temperature**
6. **Rejuvenating: make to look or feel younger, fresher, or more lively**

Chapter 14

A Very Long Hour

"Something must be wrong," Josh said. "Dad should have been here by now."

"I'm really getting scared. What should we do?" Sydney asked.

"I say we go look for him."

"But Dad told us to stay put."

"What if something happened to him," Josh insisted.

"I guess you're right. It has been a long time. I'll get my flashlight."

"One more thing, Sydney. Go to the bathroom before we leave the room.

Okay?"

"Yeah, right," Sydney agreed.

They left the room cautiously. The hallway was very dark, as the lights were still out.

"Josh, I'm afraid to go down the stairwell," Sydney confessed. "Do you suppose there might be another way down?"

"You mean, like a secret passage?"

"Yeah!"

"Hey, that might not be a bad idea! Maybe you're onto something."

They began to check every cubbyhole and corner, pushing and pulling on everything. The only door that opened along the long hallway was Room 333, Mr. Peterson's room.

"Why are we going in here?" Sydney asked.

"I don't know. But it's open, and we don't have to worry about anyone being in here since Mr. Peterson is dead. Let's just look around."

They searched through Mr. Peterson's things again. Everything was pretty much as before. As expected, his hunting *attire* was gone, since he had gone hunting, and his rifle and some shells were missing. Other than that, everything was the same.

- **Attire: clothes, especially fine or formal ones**

"What are you doing, Josh?"

"I'm trying the window," he said, straining to open it. "It opens!"

"So? I don't think you call that a secret passage. A window is a normal opening."

"Yes, but don't you remember, Mr. Peterson said that Bill Clark changed rooms with him because the window wouldn't open. Someone wanted him in this room. Why?" Josh then looked out of the window and down below. "Look for yourself, Sydney.There's a metal ladder that goes down to the second floor."

Both were hanging out the window, marveling at their discovery. The snow continued to fall, causing the ladder to be very slippery. They would have to leave their flashlight off, lest someone see them.

"Okay, I'm going first. You follow," Josh instructed.

But before he could make his exit, they heard the turn of the doorknob. They hid behind the long, thick, dusty drapes that covered the open window. Josh regretted he could not close the window. He only hoped the intruder would not notice the window was now open. From the sounds of it, the *intruder* was going through Peterson's things, seemingly looking for something. They held their breath as the intruder neared the window. The footsteps echoed in their ears, becoming louder and louder, as they approached the window. It felt as though their hearts were beating in their throats. Then the thing they feared the most happened. Sydney was grabbed by the arm and pulled from behind the curtain by the prowler. She let out a scream, but it was obviously muffled by a firm hand placed over her mouth. Josh had to make a decision quickly. He could run for his life by way of the window, or he would have to fight for his sister. The room was dark, as the lights were still out. Josh could not see a thing, but he decided to battle for Sydney. He came out kicking and yelling, "Let go of my sister! Don't you hurt her!"

"I would never hurt her," the man said tenderly, breathing a sigh of relief.

"Dad!" Josh exclaimed.

Jake was holding on to Sydney with his left arm. *Instinctively*, Josh reached out to hug him on his right side, where he had been wounded. Jake groaned, letting go of Sydney, and grabbing his wounded arm in a protective manner.

- **Intruder: person who intrudes**
- **Instinctively: without conscious thought, by natural instinct**

"Dad! What happened? You've been hurt," Sydney said.

"I'll tell you all about it when we get back to my room. From now on, you kids are not leaving my sight. Now help me back to my room. I'm so sleepy."

"Dad, what are you doing in Mr. Peterson's room, anyway?" Josh asked.

"I might ask you the same thing. What are you doing here, when I asked you to stay put?"

"We were looking for you," Sydney explained. "And I was looking for you two."

"Guess what? We found a secret passage!" Josh said.

"A secret passage? That's very interesting," he said, rubbing his chin, tilting his head to the right. He then looked out the window to see this discovery of theirs. He pulled his head back into the room, laughing heartily. "A very interesting ladder, indeed! With snow falling as heavy as it is, I suppose a drainage pipe held up by wires could resemble a ladder."

"A drainage pipe?!" they cried in unison.

"Yeah, a good old-fashioned gutter! Now, come on my little sleuths, before we call attention to ourselves."

"Okay Dad, but we'll have to stay in my room," Sydney insisted.

"Why is that, Sydney?"

"Because my clothes and makeup are there."

Jake continued to laugh with a deep *guttural* laugh. "Okay, then we'll stay in your room. Heaven forbid you should be separated from such basic essentials."

- **Guttural: sound produced in the throat**

Once inside the room, Jake O'Neal took some shells out of his pocket. "Josh, I want you to watch me load this rifle. It's not difficult but pay attention. Then, I want to see you do it. Sydney, I would show you, but I know you could never pull the trigger, even if your life depended on it."

After watching Josh finish loading the rifle, he made a quick search of the room, then fell back onto the bed. His eyes were very heavy. He fought back the yawns as he had not finished giving his kids instructions.

"Josh, wake me up in one hour. Don't let me sleep later than that. We will all be meeting downstairs, in the diner. One hour, no more than that. And Josh ...."

"Yes, Dad?"

"Use the rifle, if you have too. And Sydney ... " he said, his eyes heavy with sleep, "1 need to see ... the blowups of the body. Have them ready, when I wake ...."

His left arm then fell off the side of the bed and he went peacefully to sleep. They covered him with blankets. Josh pulled up a chair, sitting with his legs crossed in pretzel style. With rifle in hand, he faced the door. He would use it if he had too. Sydney prayed he wouldn't have too. It would be a very long hour.

Chapter 14 Definitions Review

1. **Attire: clothes, especially fine or formal ones**
2. **Intruder: person who intrudes**
3. **Instinctively: without conscious thought, by natural instinct**
4. **Guttural: sound produced in the throat**

Chapter 15

Dead or Alive

"Dad," Josh said, with a gentle whisper. Jake O'Neal just grunted, ignoring his gentle nudges.

"Let him sleep. He looks so tired. And I think he's got a fever. He's been sweating up a storm," Sydney said, applying compresses to his forehead.

"No! Dad made me promise to wake him in an hour. Dad," he whispered again.

"It's almost midnight. Wake up, Dad!" Josh patted his face and shook his shoulder. He slowly opened his eyes. They were glossy with fever. His cheeks were flushed. He winced in pain, as he tried to get up.

"Help me up, Josh," he said. His voice was weak.

"Dad, you're not well," Sydney argued.

"I'll be alright," he said, giving Sydney a forced smile. "I just need a little help to get going. Get me a glass of water, please."

Sydney quickly got him a cool glass of water. He took something out of his shirt pocket, put it in his mouth, and chased it down with the water. After sitting on the side of the bed for about ten minutes, he got up, washed his face, combed his hair, and came back looking somewhat revived.

"Sydney, do you have the blowups of the body?"

"Yeah, would you like to see them now?"

"Great job, Sydney," her dad said, flashing the light on the pictures. "This is exactly what I expected. Now let's go down to the diner and solve this mystery."

The lights were still out. The diner was lit with candles and lanterns. Everyone was there. Everyone, that is except for Peterson, Clark, Joe Strange, and of course, the Whites. Fred Moore was still in front of the fireplace, lying on a bear skin rug, being nursed by Sarah. Color had returned to his face. Sarah continued to give him sips of warm liquids. Thomas Stevenson sat in a rocker with his rifle in ready position. Carl Young was at a table playing with a deck of cards, chewing on the butt of a cigar. Scott McCauley and Paul Pierce stood at the fireplace, each with rifle in hand. Mr. Roberts was at another table sitting with the two maids. Jake, Josh, and Sydney took seats at a table near the fireplace.

"Well, if it's not John Wayne returning with one young prince and one young *damsel* in distress," Sarah said.

"John Wayne? I think she is talking about you, Dad," Sydney said, puzzled at the comment.

"Your father refused to rest until he saw that you two were safe. I told him you were, but he had to see for himself. He rested for a whole ten minutes after I gave him enough medicine to knock out a horse. He's got a pretty nasty wound to that arm. Let me see it," Sarah said, reaching for his arm.

"Sarah, quit worrying over me. I know you mean well, but I'm fine. Really."

"A wolf bite can be pretty serious, young man!" Sarah scolded.

"A wolf bite!" They cried out in *unison*.

"You said you met up with a little trouble, not a wolf," Josh said.

- **Damsel: a young unmarried woman**
- **Unison: simultaneous performance of action or utterance of speech**

"Well, that's what I named the wolf, Trouble. Now, stop all this fuss. We have a murder mystery to solve," Jake said, taking control of the meeting. "Ladies and gentlemen, today two bodies were found. Out on a hunting *excursion*, the body of Mr. Charles Peterson was found at the bottom of the cliff. Was it an accident? Or was he murdered? I say it was no accident, and I feel I have positive proof. I was brought here by Mr. Peterson. He felt that there was a threat on his life. He wanted me here to flush out his would-be killer.

Gentlemen, there is a killer among us."

The executives became very attentive to the words of Jake O'Neal. All eyes were upon him.

"Of course, you are referring to Joe Strange," Mr. Roberts offered.

"Yes, and no," Jake said.

"Speak clearly, O'Neal. What are you saying?" Paul Pierce asked. "Is it Joe Strange or not?"

"I think Joe Strange is just a part of this mystery. There is the mastermind behind Joe Strange. Mr. Peterson was concerned that someone in his organization was out to get him."

"Who are you accusing, O'Neal?" Carl Young asked.

"I'm not accusing anyone. We will let the facts speak for themselves."

"If anyone had a motive, it's you, Fred. Your job was on the line," Mr. Young said, pointing his cigar at him.

Fred Moore pulled himself up, grabbing his left shoulder in pain. Sarah continued doting over him, propping his head on her lap.

"Easy now," she cajoled, rubbing his brow.

"Yeah, right. So, I went and got myself shot. Why?" Fred said, raising his voice in anger.

"It would make a good *alibi*," Mr. Roberts offered. "It would certainly throw the authorities off the trail."

- **Excursion: a short journey or trip**
- **Alibi: evidence that someone was somewhere else when a crime occurred**

"What about you, Carl? You had gambling debts," Thomas Stevenson interjected. "Your job wasn't that secure either."

"Wait a minute," Jake said. "Let's bring out all the facts. First of all, this is the perfect place for a crime, far away from civilization. It had to be chosen specifically with this in mind. It couldn't have been planned better."

"Then it was Carl. He chose this God forsaken place. He doesn't hunt. He doesn't even ski. Why else would he pick a place like this?" Paul Pierce accused.

"But he wasn't on the hunt with us," Scott McCauley argued.

"But he did go out. He admitted to that," Jake said.

"I only went out because I wanted to see who would nail the first deer. I was going to wager a bet on who shot the first deer. But I never made it up there. It started to snow. And, it was too *strenuous* for me, so I turned around. I swear! Besides, look at me. I couldn't have moved that fast and gotten back to the Lodge before you," he said in his defense.

- **Strenuous: requiring or using great exertion**

"I always knew you were a cheat!" Moore said. "And you could have made it back in time if you had access to the snowmobile. Or you could have had Joe Strange do your dirty work. How did you know about this place anyway?"

"Before we go any further, I want to submit this flyer as our first piece of evidence. It's an advertisement for the Lodge. I found it in Carl Young's room. We'll call it exhibit A," Jake said, holding the piece of paper by the lantern, for everyone to see.

Then he laid it on the table before him.

"Let's hear you explain that one, Carl," Scott McCauley insisted.

"The flyer simply came through my email one day. You know good and well what a tightwad Peterson was. I had a limited budget to work with. Peterson told me that if I kept the cost down, I would get a bonus. See for yourselves. The price couldn't be beat. So, who cares if I don't ski or hunt, I got a bonus. Everyone was happy," Carl said.

"Especially the killer," Jake added.

"What do you mean?" Carl Young asked.

"Don't you see, whoever sent you that email knew that you were the one to set up this trip and was playing into your hand,"

Jake answered.

"Who sent the email?" Stevenson asked.

"I don't really know," Carl said, picking up the email to study it.

"For exhibit B, I have a letter of **reprimand** from Charles Peterson to Fred Moore. It seems, Mr. Moore, that you were taking on more responsibility than was allotted you," Jake said.

"I've been with the company a lot longer than Charles Peterson. I should have been the CEO. I don't know what he did to convince the board that he should be in charge. I was the better man for the job. And he brought in that young, inexperienced Bill Clark, telling everyone that he would be the next president of the company," Fred said, becoming short winded.

"Lay back. You need your rest. You are using up all your energy. Don't get all worked up," Sarah insisted.

"Lady, I'm being accused of murder. And you want me to sit back and relax?!" "Did you kill Bill, too?" Paul Pierce asked, his eyes were blaring with rage.

"I didn't kill anyone! But they both deserved it, if you ask me. Besides, if I would have killed anyone, I would have used a gun," Fred said, struggling for breath. He was **obviously** tiring. "I wouldn't use poison, or push him off a cliff, like a coward."

- **Reprimand: rebuke**
- **Obvious: easily perceived or understood, clear**

"Where were you anyway when Peterson fell off the cliff," Scott McCauley asked.

"You mean when he was pushed," Paul Pierce corrected.

"I left you all in the brush, and I doubled back. I wanted to get the first deer. I didn't think it was fair for O'Neal here ... to have the advantage," Moore explained between breaths.

"And you call me a cheat?" Carl Young accused.

"Please, no one is accusing anyone. We are just bringing out facts," Jake repeated, shifting his position. His pain was obvious. He held his rifle in his left hand. His right arm was in a homemade sling. "Now, the matter of Bill Clark's death. He was poisoned. Pierce was good enough to do a drug screen on a certain liquid found in his room. Bill apparently drank from this glass prior to his death. Why don't you tell us what you found, Paul."

"It was Digoxin, a medicine that is used to strengthen, yet slow the heart down. The dose was enough to slow his heart down permanently."

"The question is, did the killer mean to kill Bill Clark, or was he aiming for Charles Peterson and missed?" Jake O'Neal said. "He may not have known that Clark and Peterson changed rooms?" Turning to the cook, he continued, "Sarah, did Bill Clark order a glass of tea to be brought up to his room this afternoon?"

"No, but Mr. Peterson did," Sarah offered.

"Did you bring it to his room?"

"I brought it to his room," Mr. Roberts volunteered.

"Which room did you bring it to?"

"Room 331, of course. Mr. Peterson said he was going to take a shower, and that I should leave it at the door. That's exactly what I did," Roberts insisted.

"Did anyone know that Peterson and Clark changed rooms?" Jake asked.

No one admitted to knowing of the switch.

"Then we can assume that the tea was meant for Charles Peterson and not for Bill Clark," Thomas Stevenson said.

"But who put the poison in the tea?" Paul Pierce asked.

"It could have been anyone," Jake said.

"What about Roberts? He had the tea in his hand," Stevenson said.

"And what motive would I have to do away with this fellow?" Mr. Roberts protested. "If you ask me, any of you being with a pharmaceutical company should have ample knowledge of poisoning an individual."

"Dad, what about the book in Mr. Stevenson's room?" Josh whispered.

"Let me handle this, Joshua," Jake said.

The Lost Lodge

"You little squirt! Were you in my room? You're a snoop, just like your dad," Thomas Stevenson said, pointing his finger at Josh in an accusing manner.

"I want to hear about the book. What did you find?" Fred asked weakly.

"The book was entitled, 'How to Commit the Perfect Crime.' There was also a lot of chemicals and rat poison in his room," Josh blurted out.

"I always knew there was a dark side to him," Carl Young said.

"So, I like murder mysteries. What's wrong with that?" Thomas Stevenson said, defending himself.

"So, he's the killer!" Paul Pierce said. He began pacing up and down. Looking around wildly.

"Look Paul, you've accused everyone so far. What about you? How do we know you aren't the one?" Stevenson asked.

"Why, you …." Paul Pierce started to say something but was cut short by Jake O'Neal.

"Let's stay on track, gentlemen," Jake said. "We need to look at all the facts before accusing anyone. Now, we come to the sudden disappearance of Joe Strange, the caretaker. Was his timely disappearance a *coincidence*? I don't think so. As I went to his room this evening, I had a close encounter with death myself. His room was booby trapped. It was a close call, and Mr. Roberts can testify to that, seeing he was the one leading me like a sheep to the slaughter."

- **Coincidence: remarkable occurrence of events or circumstances**

"I don't know what you are talking about. I was just as surprised as you were when the gun went off. Why, we were both nearly killed," Mr. Roberts said in his defense.

"Then Joe Strange has to be the killer, right, O'Neal?" Pierce asked.

"It would appear so. Or rather someone would have it appear

so," Jake answered.

"Go on. We're listening," Scott McCauley encouraged.

Jake then pulled out the evidence taken from Joe's room: the newspaper cuttings. All eyes were fixed on the new evidence. "Now, I have a question for all of you. How many of you have received a threatening note cut out of newsprint?"

All confirmed receiving such a note, this very evening, when they returned to their rooms. However, Fred Moore was unable to return to his room, so he was unaware of receiving such a note. They pulled out their notes and placed them on the table with the other exhibits.

"What does this mean O'Neal? Why would Joe Strange send us these threatening notes? We didn't even know him. You study the criminal mind. Is he just some kind of psycho?" Carl Young asked.

"It wasn't Joe Strange at all. It couldn't have been," Jake O'Neal said.

"That's right!" Josh said, catching on to where he was going. "Mr. Strange couldn't read! He couldn't read the menu at the Grill in Martinsville!"

"Exactly! But our killer didn't know that when he framed Joe Strange. The killer planned to kill all of you. He planned to hunt you down, one by one."

"But it was Joe Strange who shot me at the cabin. I saw him," Fred Moore insisted.

"Are you absolutely sure? Did you see his face?" Jake challenged.

"The snow was coming down pretty heavily, but I couldn't mistake that red hat, and yellow coat that he wore!" he said, forcing every breath out.

"Fred, do you really feel like you should have hit that deer on the hunt today?" Jake asked.

"I know I should have killed him."

"And you also think you got a good aim on Joe Strange, this evening. Is that right?"

"I know I had him." Fred Moore was very *insistent*.

"Yet, he got away. I would wager that your shells have been

replaced with blanks. Go ahead, you have your rifle, fire it," Jake said.

In spite of the protests from Mr. Roberts and Sarah, Fred Moore struggled to his feet, and with what little strength he had, he fired the rifle at a nearby windowpane. There was a loud blast, but the window did not break. Nothing happened. Sarah gave a **stern** rebuke to Jake O'Neal, then assisted Fred Moore to a supine position on the bearskin rug in front of the fire. She then propped his head up on her lap and covered him with a blanket. Mr. Moore seemed to take comfort in her tender loving care.

"All of you have your rifles, but they are worthless. Your shells have all been replaced with blanks. The killer planned to hunt you down and watch you die like defenseless animals," Jake explained.

"Now I understand why he just looked at me before he shot. He wanted me … to have ... the first … shot …. He was just … playing a game. He was … hunting me," Fred said, his voice trailing off.

"If it's not Joe Strange, then who is it?" Paul Pierce demanded.

"It's Mr. Robert White, the owner of the Lodge. He had help from his wife. And, of course, Jonathan Roberts, the clerk, and Matilda, the cook at Gary's Greasy Grill in Martinsville, were both in on it."

"We don't even know Robert White. Why would he want to kill us?" Carl Young asked.

"Why don't you ask him yourself? He's at the top of the stairs," Jake said. Then he turned to face the stairway. "I thought that shot would bring you out of hiding, Mr. White! Now why don't you come into the light so everyone can see you."

The man slowly came down the stairs. Fear was **paramount** as the men were to meet the killer face to face.

- **Insistent: insisting or demanding something**
- **Stern: serious and unrelenting**
- **Paramount: more important than anything else**

"You! But it can't be," Paul Pierce said in unbelief.

"We thought you were dead!" Scott McCauley called out.

"But, how ...." Carl Young said, his cigar falling out of his mouth.

"We saw your body," Stevenson said, looking puzzled.   .

Confusion came over the group as the man with the red hat and yellow coat came into full view. It was Charles Peterson.

"You did see a body, alright. But it wasn't mine," he said laughing.

"Then whose was it?" Scott McCauley asked.

"It was the body of Joe Strange, the caretaker," Jake answered.

"Very clever, O'Neal. How did you figure it out?" Peterson asked.

"You made a lot of mistakes. First, the flyer that advertised the Lodge had the same address of the email you sent me regarding the details of the trip. Young kept the flyer. You made the advertisement irresistible to Carl, promising him a bonus, if he kept the cost down. You knew he had gambling debts and that he needed the money. I suspected you, when I saw the newspaper clippings. My older child is a good judge of character. He took to Joe Strange right away. He was just an *ignorant* man who loved and trusted people too much. You knew he didn't have any family and that he wouldn't be missed by anyone if something happened to him. And then there's my younger daughter's excellent photography." He then pulled out the blown-up pictures of the body. "We'll call this exhibit C. I remembered seeing a tattoo of a cross below Joe's left ear. As you can see, it showed up well on the blowup. You hand-picked Joe Strange to take your place in death, using Matilda, your sister-in-law, to lure him over here through the internet. Your real name is Robert White. You own all the property here and the grill in Martinsville. Matilda, your sister-in-law, Jonathan Roberts' wife, posed as the cook. She built a relationship with Joe through the internet and brought him to the lodge. You planned, from the beginning, for him to take your place in death. He had your same build, red hair, and he had no family. What you didn't know was that Joe could not read or write. He had a friend who did all the corresponding with Matilda. He could not have sent those threatening notes."

"That bumbling idiot! He deserved to die. The *audacity* of such a crude person to think that my Matilda could love such a one as he," Jonathan Roberts said.

- **Ignorant: lacking knowledge or awareness, uneducated**
- **Audacity: willingness to take bold risks**

"I must say, O'Neal, I underestimated you. You are better at this game than I had imagined," Charles Peterson said. "However did you figure all of this out?"

"I had help. I discovered Bill Clark's diary. It was in some kind of code. He was on to you. I cracked his code, which wasn't very difficult. I discovered some valuable information. You knew Bill was on to you, too. That's why you tried to kill him. There was nothing wrong with his window. My kids can verify that," he smiled at his children, who stood by his side, proudly supporting him. "You brought Bill the tea, after the rooms were switched. You put the Digoxin in it. You were taking Digoxin for a bad heart. I saw a bottle in your room."

"Correction! I didn't try to kill Bill Clark. I did!" Peterson said.

"Correction!" A voice from the top of the stairs called out.

"Bill!" Mr. Peterson exclaimed.

"Why, you look like you've seen a ghost, Mr. Peterson. Or, should I say, Mr. White?" Bill said, taking his place next to Jake.

"How ... but, you ...." Mr. Peterson stumbled over his words.

"I never drank the tea. I knew you had planned something when you asked me to change rooms. I didn't order any tea. I figured it had to be a plan to poison me. You tried to kill me just like you killed Uncle Jamison," Bill said.

"Jed Jamison was your uncle!?" Moore asked, confused. "He was a fine man. But, he died of a heart attack."

"Who is Jed Jamison?" Josh asked, not wanting to be left in the dark.

"Jamison was the CEO of Brexler Labs before Peterson took

over. Bill Clark was in Europe when his uncle died. By the time he got back to the States, his body had been cremated. Mrs. Jamison never trusted Charles Peterson. She insisted that Mr. Peterson had something to do with his death because of some of the things her husband had said about him. So, over the past few years, Bill has worked his way up to the executive level to try to solve this mystery. No one knew he was Jamison's nephew," Jake said.

"But Dad! Mr. Clark looked dead! He was cold, and blue, and ...." Sydney exclaimed.

"We decided to make the killer think he was dead. Bill took a heavy dose of sleeping pills, being careful to make sure it wasn't a lethal dose. So, he looked pretty limp and lifeless. As for being cold, no one touched him, but me. Very few people will touch a dead body. And Sydney, I hope you don't mind, but I borrowed a little of your makeup to make him look a little *ashen*."

- **Ashen: pale gray color of ash**

"So, that's where all my blue eye shadow went."

"See! I told you, it wasn't me!" exclaimed Josh.

"Well, how was I to know that Dad would use it?"

"What is this, a makeup party or something?! You think you outsmarted me, but you didn't. Now you're all going to die. It's time for me to take my revenge. The day has finally come," Peterson bellowed.

"Don't we have a right to know why we're going to die?" Stevenson asked. His voice was steady.

"I think you owe them that much," Jake agreed.

"Shut up, O'Neal! I don't owe anybody anything. They owe me! We're just evening the score."

"I suppose you hired me to throw off any suspicion from yourself," Jake said.

"That's right. And it would have worked out fine. But you had to keep digging and snooping. Now, I'm going to have to do away with you and your two junior snoops."

"If I'm going to die, I have a right to know why!" Josh demanded.

"Be quiet, Josh! He's a wild man with a gun!" Sydney pleaded.

"You're a spunky one. Aren't you?" Mr. Peterson said, a strange, yet saddened expression coming over his face. Josh looked at him with pity as he gazed into his eyes. "I had a son once. He was about your age. He was my life. We enjoyed hunting together. We would come here, to this very place, every winter. This was our favorite place to hunt. I haven't hunted since his death fifteen years ago."

"What happened to him," Josh asked tenderly.

"He was stricken with a rare disease. The only medicine that could help him was still in the research stage. A medicine that is now on the market and made by Brexler Labs. A medicine that I helped research when I was just a nobody in the company. A medicine I begged for to be used experimentally on my son, Bobby. It was Jamison who denied me. No, he didn't know me personally. I went through every avenue I knew. I wrote letters. I pleaded with countless supervisors. And everyone told me the same thing, The drug was in the experimental phase, and we could not use it. My son died. He didn't have a chance. He lasted only three months. Six months later, the drug went on the market and is now saving lives. It could have saved my son's life. Brexler Labs killed my son! They killed me too! I changed my name and worked my way to the top. Yes, I killed Jamison, and I took his place. Now, I'm going to kill the rest of you!" He then burst out into violent laughter. He was a mad man, full of bitterness and rage.

"Mr. Peterson, killing us won't bring your son back," Josh said very softly, taking a step toward him.

"He looked at Josh very tenderly. He reached over and placed his hand on Josh's shoulder. Josh did not flinch, but stood tall, and tried his best to smile. He knew this man was hurting. He had to be very careful not to pour salt on his wound. "Tell me about your son, Mr. Peterson. I'll bet you were very proud of him."

"I was," he said with a weakened voice.

"Don't listen to him! We've come too far to turn back now!" a female voice said.

The tall blonde woman was coming down the stairs, with a lantern in hand. It was Mrs. White, or rather Mrs. Peterson. She was a beautiful woman, yet her countenance reeked of bitterness. She took her place next to Mr. Peterson. Accompanying her was Matilda, the cook from the Greasy Grill, who took her place next to Jonathan Roberts, her husband. The four of them glared at the group like vultures, ready to pick their *prey*.

•   **Prey: an animal that is hunted**

"You might as well meet the rest of the family. This is my wife, Margaret, and her twin sister, Matilda. And, of course, you already know my brother-in-law, Jonathan Roberts. Together, we are judge, jury, and executioner. And we find you all guilty!"

"Go ahead and kill them, like they killed my son!" Margaret shouted.

"Let their families feel the grief we have felt as a family for so many years," Jonathan Roberts said.

"Yes, let them suffer as we have suffered," Matilda agreed with her husband.

Mr. Peterson then pointed his gun at Mr. Moore. "You're going first."

Jake O'Neal pointed his rifle at Mr. Peterson. "Drop your gun, Peterson. It's no use. You've been found out."

"You're forgetting, O'Neal, I put blanks in your gun and all of their guns. Don't you remember me asking you, that day I visited your house, what kind of ammunition you used? I have planned well. I'm afraid you're defenseless. Besides, how good a shot could you be with a busted right arm?"

At once, McCauley and Stevenson both lifted their rifles to shoot. 'Blam!' the rifles sounded, but nothing happened.

Peterson laughed savagely. "You just couldn't resist it, could you? I told you, I put blanks in all your guns!"

Carl Young stood up, his whole body visibly shaking. He pulled out a revolver and aimed it at Charles Peterson. "I bet you didn't put blanks in my gun! I bet you didn't even know I owned a gun."

Charles Peterson looked amused at what he was looking at. "What is that? A toy gun?"

"Don't make me do it, Peterson! I'll shoot!" Carl Young said.

"You're a coward. You won't shoot. I'm going to enjoy seeing you squirm like the worm you are."

"Shoot!" Paul Pierce yelled. "Shoot, Carl!"

Carl Young pulled the trigger. 'Click!' the gun sounded but did not fire. At the failure of the gun to fire, Young fell on his knees, begging and sobbing. "Please! Don't shoot me. I'll give you anything you want. You can have all my money."

"That's one bet you lost. I took the gun powder out of your bullets. I put blanks in everybody else's rifles. When I found your gun, I almost didn't even waste my time with it. Frankly, I didn't think you had the guts to pull the trigger. What are you doing with a gun anyway?" Peterson asked.

"I brought it for protection. I'm afraid of bears!"

Mr. Peterson roared with laughter at that comment. "Carl, you are stupid if you thought that little toy gun could save you from a bear." He then turned to Jake O'Neal, "Now, you're going first. You nearly messed up my plans. Now, I'm going to get you out of the way. Look at it this way, O'Neal, I will be putting you out of your misery. You're obviously wounded. Gangrene will probably set in by morning. A wolf bite without medical attention is deadly. This way will be a lot easier. And don't worry about your wonderful kids. I'll make sure their deaths are easy and painless. You can all be buried together. Isn't that how you would want it?"

With madness in his eyes, he then pulled his rifle up and went for Jake O'Neal. There was a sudden flash of blinding light followed by a blast from a rifle, then a thump to the floor. A second shot sounded, and then a second thump to the floor. Massive confusion went through the diner as a fight for survival commenced. There was shuffling and clamor, screams and grunts. Tables were overturned, causing the candles to go out of the already dimly lit room. Then, all went silent. Flickering lights came on one by one, as Sarah relit the candles.

"Dad!" Josh screamed, running over to where he lay supine on the floor. His eyes were closed. Josh put his head on his dad's chest. He did not see the rise and fall of his chest. He didn't hear or feel his breath. Sydney stood over them in a state of shock, not able to move or speak. Tears were running down her cheeks. Josh felt warm blood running down his chest and onto his hand.

"Dad, please don't die," he pleaded, sobbing deeply. "Oh God, please don't take my dad. Please, God."

Meanwhile, Thomas Stevenson had recovered Charles Peterson's rifle after he had been shot. He held the group at bay with Peterson's rifle, while holding a foot on Peterson's chest. Peterson had been shot in the leg, knocking him off his feet.

"Let me see what I can do," Bill Clark said to Josh, pulling him away from Jake O'Neal. Lifting Jake's chin to make sure his airway was open, Bill felt for a pulse. He could not feel or hear respirations. He knew what he had to do. He knew CPR. He proceeded to do mouth to mouth resuscitation, giving him a great big breath. He could see the rise and fall of his chest, as the breath went in. He then repeated the action. Jake began to cough, spit, and sputter.

"Man! What are you doing?!" Jake asked, looking a bit disgusted.

"I'm saving your life. What does it look like?" Bill replied, wiping his mouth on his sleeve.

"Just as long as you're not kissing me!" he said, protecting his manhood.

Josh and Sydney threw themselves on him, showering him with hugs and kisses.

"Oww!" Jake groaned. "Watch the arm!"

"Dad, you're bleeding. You've been shot!" Sydney said.

"No, I'm not shot. The arm wound just opened up again in the scuffle."

"Dad, I thought you were going to die!" Josh said, holding onto him tightly.

"No, I'm not going to die. Not yet, anyway. I just got the wind knocked out of me from the scuffle and falling on the floor. I guess

I'm weaker than I thought. Now help me up."

Bill helped Jake onto his feet. Together they moved to where Thomas Stevenson held a gun to Charles Peterson.

"Don't worry, Peterson. You're not going to die either. Not at my hand anyway. It's just a flesh wound," Jake said, holding the barrel of his rifle on him.

Mr. Peterson lay on the floor, his head on his wife's lap, as she cried violently. McCauley and Pierce had **apprehended** Jonathan Roberts and his wife.

"But I put blanks in your gun," Peterson said, weakened and defeated.

"I happened to remember that you and I both used a 30-30 caliber rifle, and a 150 grain bullet. So, I went by your room and borrowed a few bullets from you. By that time, I figured out that you had substituted blanks in everyone's rifles. And these were no ordinary blanks. They were well crafted to make them look like the real thing. I knew you wouldn't have blanks for your own rifle. I counted on it. And I was right. What's ironic is I shot you with your own bullet. And, by the way, if you had paid more attention, you would have noticed that I usually shoot **southpaw**. But, for future reference I am also **ambidextrous**, so I can shoot just as well south paw or right-handed."

- **Apprehended: arrest for a crime**
- **Southpaw: left-handed person**
- **Ambidextrous: able to use right and left hand equally well**

"So, that's what you were doing in Mr. Peterson's room when you found us," Josh said.

"You mean, when you found your secret passage?" Jake smiled and winked at Josh.

"What secret passage?" Peterson asked. "I don't know of any secret passage. Do you, Margaret?"

"Why didn't you kill him when you had the chance," Margaret scolded her husband. "He's ruined everything!"

"I was blinded by a flash of light. I don't know where it came from," he said.

"It was Sydney's camera," Josh volunteered.

"That was quick thinking," Bill said to Sydney. "That flash of your camera was split second timing, throwing Peterson off, and giving your dad just enough time to make a quick but accurate shot."

"Oh, it was nothing," Sydney said, throwing her hair back, revealing her blushing cheeks.

"I knew you had it in you," Josh said, giving his sister a big bear hug.

"Stevenson, what do you say we make a make-shift jail until morning. Would you take the first watch?" Jake asked.

"I'd be happy to oblige you," he said with a *sinister* smile.

"Sarah, do you think you can serve up some grub? If you recall, some of us didn't make it for supper."

"I will, right after I tend that wound and clean up this place."

"Dad, Mr. Peterson said that *gangrene* would set in your arm by morning. Is that true?" Sydney asked, worry written all over her face.

- **Sinister: giving the impression of something harmful or evil is happening or will happen**
- **Gangrene: decomposition of body tissue**

"I don't think you need to worry about that," Bill offered. "I have had extensive medical training. I've already started your dad on *antibiotics*. He came to see me on his way to see you kids. I also gave him some adrenalin to counteract any ill effects from Sarah's potion, since we weren't sure if she was in on this fiasco or not."

The Lost Lodge

- **Antibiotics: medicine that inhibits the growth of microorganisms**

"From the way she dawdles over Fred, I would say she is definitely a friend and not a foe," Jake said.

"That's for sure! He shouldn't feel neglected," Bill said.

"Bill, would you join me and my kids for supper?"

"You bet! I feel like I haven't eaten in a week."

"Dad," Sydney whispered, walking to the table with her father as Bill and Josh followed them.

"Yes, Sydney. What is it?"

"Do you remember what I said about Bill Clark in his room? You know, when I thought he was dead?"

"About him being cute?" Dad said, laughter in his voice.

"Yes," she said, timidly.

"Yes, I remember very well."

"Do you think he heard me?"

"Sydney, that's one mystery I'll leave for you to solve. As for me, this case is closed!"

Chapter 15 Definitions Review

1. **Damsel:** a young unmarried woman
2. **Unison:** simultaneous performance of action or utterance of speech
3. **Excursion:** a short journey or trip
4. **Alibi:** evidence that someone was somewhere else when a crime occurred
5. **Strenuous:** requiring or using great exertion
6. **Reprimand:** rebuke
7. **Obvious:** easily perceived or understood, clear
8. **Coincidence:** remarkable occurrence of events or circumstances
9. **Insistent:** insisting or demanding something
10. **Stern:** serious and unrelenting
11. **Paramount:** more important than anything else
12. **Ignorant:** lacking knowledge or awareness, uneducated
13. **Audacity:** willingness to take bold risks
14. **Ashen:** pale gray color of ash
15. **Prey:** an animal that is hunted
16. **Apprehended:** arrest for a crime
17. **Southpaw:** left-handed person
18. **Ambidextrous:** able to use right and left hand equally well
19. **Sinister:** giving the impression of something harmful or evil is happening or will happen
20. **Gangrene:** decomposition of body tissue
21. **Antibiotics:** medicine that prevents the growth of microorganisms (germs)

The Conclusion

The plane ride home was a time of reflection. The blizzard had subsided. Mr. Peterson and his family had been apprehended by the authorities, and it was time for the O'Neals to return home. Sydney had the window seat this time. She stared out idly. Josh's brows came together as they did when he was really concentrating on something. Mr. O'Neal looked at both his kids, grateful for their safety.

"You look so serious, Josh. What's going through that handsome little head of yours?"

"I was thinking about Mom in the hospital the night she died and one of the last things she said to me," Josh said, his eyes welling up with tears.

"Yes, go on ..." Jake O'Neal encouraged his son to talk.

"I was so angry at the drunk driver that hit her. I hated him. Mom made me promise to forgive him. She said it was so important that I do. She said that if I didn't forgive him, I would become like him, hurting others, and then hurting myself. I really never understood that until Mr. Peterson. He was hurt when his son died. He didn't forgive those who he thought were responsible for his son's death. He became bitter and look what happened. He killed and hurt others, and then he hurt himself and his family. He lost everything. It was very hard for me to forgive that drunk driver. I did it for Mom. Now, I'm glad I did. Mr. Peterson's life could have been so different had he forgiven."

"It looks like you've learned a very valuable lesson, Josh. Mom would be very proud of you. I certainly am."

The plane began to descend as they approached the airport in Dallas.

"Dad, I need to go to the bathroom," Sydney demanded.

"It's too late. We're descending. You need to stay in your seatbelt. We'll be on the ground shortly."

"But, Dad ..." Sydney insisted.

"No buts, Sydney. You will just have to wait. It's too dangerous," Jake O'Neal instructed.

Sydney turned very pale, and before she could turn away, she vomited right into Josh's lap. "Josh, I'm so sorry. I tried to go to the bathroom ... "

"Sydney Reese! Not again!" Josh exclaimed.